THE BLACK TERRORIST

TIERNO MONÉNEMBO

THE BLACK TERRORIST

TIERNO MONÉNEMBO

Translated by C. Dickson

DIASPORIC AFRICA PRESS
NEW YORK

This book is a publication of
Diasporic Africa Press
New York | www.dafricapress.com

Library of Congress Control Number: 2015956286
ISBN-13 978-1-937306-36-6 (pbk.: alk paper)

Cover photo credit: Addi Bâ , ca. 1940
(© E. Guillermond, http://addiba.free.fr)

DEDICATION

In memory of Hadja Bintou, my mother,
of Nénan Bhôyi,
of Nénan Mawdho,
of Néné Biro,
of Néné Diami Tanta,
of Julien Condé,
of Boyla Boyinga
of Théogène Karabayinda

For Sarsan Tierno, Tierno Macka,
Alpha Saliou, and Karamoko Mamadou.

For all Senegalese Tirailleurs, living or dead.

With gratitude to Anne-Marie and to Etienne Guillermond
as well as everyone from Tollaincourt.

On fleurit les tombes, on réchauffe le Soldat inconnu,
Vous, mes frères obscurs, personne ne vous nomme.

(Flowers are laid upon graves, a flame burns for the Unknown Soldier,
You, my invisible brothers, no one utters your names.)

—Leopold Sédar Senghor

THE BLACK TERRORIST

Did anyone tell you that before he came to Romaincourt, no one had ever seen a black man before, except the Colonel, for whom the heart of Africa and the belly of the Orient held no secrets? No? Really? You must at least have heard about all the commotion it stirred up back in those days, due to the Jerries, the Wops, the *Angliches*, the Yankees, and a bunch of other people who all held a grudge against France, and who'd decided, God only knows why, to turn the world upside down just to rankle this country. Bedlam, Mister, the grand schemozzle, as they say in our parts! Bits of Lorraine in Prussia, Latvia stuck on to Siam, shards of Czechoslovakia all over the place, Kanaks at the North Pole, Laplanders near the Equator, and him, lost out here in the back country of the Vosges, a place he'd never heard of until several months after we'd found him lying half-dead at the edge of the Bois de Chenois.

Yes, Mister, it was the World War, that dreadful state of affairs or *chale avvaire*, as Mâmiche Léontine used to call it. She, who after sixty years in Lorraine, hadn't lost a bit of her Sundgau accent. You must have heard about it—no one could have missed that, even all the way over in your country on the banks of the Limpopo.

The Valdenaires were the first ones to set eyes on him, Mister—the father and his son—it was the time of year when meadow saffron blooms! They were out gathering golden chanterelles when suddenly the son let out a yelp, surprised by what sounded like an animal having its throat cut. He closed his eyes and pointed at a dark and disturbing heap sprawled in a thicket of whitebeams, where the earth seemed a bit less muddy. The father started, ran over, large beads of sweat bathing his face, then quickly regained his composure.

"Calm down, Etienne, it's only some poor black man."

"A German spy, then!"

"The Germans haven't got any more Negroes, and that's what started this war.... Come along, son!"

"But, Father..."

"Keep quiet, Etienne!"

The Germans had just bombed Epinal, and I, Germaine Tergoresse, still knew nothing about your uncle. Didn't know that his name was Addi Bâ and that he'd just escaped from a garrison in Neufchâteau. Above all, I had no idea that a few months later he would be living in that house you see over there, just across the way, turning my family's whole life upside down and leaving a permanent mark on the history of this town.

That unusual encounter with the Valdenaires was what started it all. I didn't witness the scene, but I know it took place at the end of September, that dismal fall when bombs were exploding under the hooves of deer, and wolfdogs would come whining up to the doors of houses. Ring any doorbell and they'll describe him better than if Renoir had filmed him: his short stature, his skin the color of castor beans, his button nose and catlike eyes, the Tirailleur uniform stained with sweat and mud, the whitebeams under which he lay, the smell of peat, and the grunting of wild boars under the chestnut trees.

It takes a lot of chance incidents to make up a life, doesn't it? Just think, had none of it ever happened, had Etienne obeyed his father, I wouldn't be here going on about your uncle. But as fate would have it, later on at the dinner table, just as he was tucking in to his *tofaille*, a ham and potato bake, his mouth had opened as if of its own accord, blurting out in a single volley, "So are we going to leave that black man in the forest, Father?"

And yet every fiber in his being had knotted together to form a sturdy net in an attempt to hold that question back. At least that's what he'd thought. He'd succeeded in doing so on the long path leading homeward and even the whole time it took him to draw the water, dig up the vegetables from the garden, collect the charcoal, and light the fire. Then the dam had broken with such force that he was relieved, in spite of his father's stricken face. Yes, he felt relieved of that burden rather than regretful about the enormous blunder he'd just committed. In the seventeen years of his life on earth, he'd never behaved in such a way. To speak to Papa like that in front of Mama at the dinner table and while there was a war raging outside!

"You've got a black man in the forest, Hubert?"

His mother's voice had the same tone as on ordinary days, neutral and calm, but with a slight inflection that hinted at something vaguely tragic and shocking.

"You're hiding something from me, Hubert Valdenaire!"

The chores, the distant respect with which they addressed one another, the dark clothing, the shuffle of wooden clogs, the long silences punctuated with wheezing and panting, had always marked the rhythm of life in the house, but young Etienne knew that when his mother said "Hubert Valdenaire," nothing was right with the world.

His mother stood up suddenly, while his father sat gloomily chewing on a crust of bread spread with Brouère cheese.

A few minutes later, while he was out in the garden, hurrying to get the tools put away and close up the chicken coop, he heard—for the very first time—loud voices coming from his parents' room. After having put the baskets and wheelbarrow into the shed, his intense curiosity kept him awake, and he put his ear to the floor of his room in the attic to better hear the whispers coming from downstairs.

"It would be sheer madness and you know it."

"You wouldn't have said that twenty years ago."

"All right, so I've changed, is that a sin?"

"He's wearing a French uniform."

"They've burned down entire villages for less than that."

"He's going to die, Hubert!"

"Then let him die!"

A long silence ensued, interrupted by the usual comings and goings: coughs, hiccups, wheezing, and the father's febrile hand rummaging in the medicine chest trying to find his pills.

"What I want is to live without bombs, without Jerries, and above all without black men. Might as well look things straight in the face."

"The face I'm looking at is pretty sorry."

Then, after mulling it over for a while, he said, "That poor man doesn't have a chance. The village still does. We're at war, Yolande."

"Then I'll be the one to go and get him."

"Fine then, go ahead!"

Other strange noises, more rapid, more agitated. Young Etienne heard footsteps crunching in the courtyard gravel, the heavy metal gate opening and closing, and the sickly voice of his father echoing in the night.

"Just some clothing and food then, nothing more! Go wake up the boy, tell him to bring the flashlight. Tell him to get the rifle too. Try and find my boots, my cap, and my scarf!"

They found him just where they'd left him—under the whitebeams—now looking even stranger, more disquieting and unreal in the wavering light of the torch. It was evident he hadn't budged in all that time. He lay still, despite his hollow groaning, as resolute and imperturbable as if he'd surrendered himself to his fate. He'd become indifferent as to whether he would die from hunger, from the cold, from the Germans, from the collaborators, or from just some peasant wanting to settle a score with a darn Negro who'd dared drag himself that far.

"Do you speak French?" ventured Hubert as he helped the boy set down the basket of food.

The question remained unanswered but, strangely enough, it silenced the man's groans.

"Do you speak French?"

The father's voice had lost all conviction. He knew the man wouldn't answer. He moved a step or two closer while Etienne was unpacking the basket. The man didn't stir; that reassured them. They couldn't explain it, but they knew he was still alive. If he were dead, they would have somehow sensed it—the smell of the earth, the rustling of the trees, the rippling of the air, something at once familiar and unusual would have convinced them of it.

Etienne extended the loaf of bread, and their eyes met for the first time, and for the first time that dark face, that clear gaze, that calm and obstinate soul, suddenly swept into his being and lodged there for all time.

The black man ate the cheese and the chicken, emptied the bottle of Contrexéville mineral water, but obstinately refused the pork and the wine. Young Etienne almost told him, "One can't afford to be picky in your condition," but he let it go. He thought it must have been because the peculiar situation, equally pathetic and unexpected, had given rise to feelings of compassion within him. Later he would realize it was because he'd just met the most unforgettable man he would encounter in the course of his lifetime.

So he simply put the slice of bacon and the jug of wine back in the basket; then he held out the sleeping bag, the quilt, and the sweater in silence.

"Do you speak French?"

At last the man was able to open his mouth and utter, "How far are we from Chaumont?"

Hubert didn't answer. He was still contemplating the words the poor devil had just spoken and the tone of his voice, like that of a child, a precocious child already invested with the magnetic and impenetrable serenity peculiar to warriors and madmen. A voice—despite its slight twang—that was filled with imposing serenity, a voice that from that moment onward has haunted our lands from the blue hills you can see over yonder all the way out to the banks of the Marne.

But the black man repeated the question no one had even thought to answer.

"What? You're thinking of trying to reach Chaumont? Preposterous! You should consider yourself lucky to have gotten this far alive. The best thing would be for you to stay here till the end of the war."

At that point the man stood up, staggered, almost fell flat on his back, managed to grab on to a branch and shake out his greatcoat, heavy with mud and rain.

"I'd rather die there than here."

He hesitated a moment and added, "Lacks a bit of sunshine around here."

"See, Etienne? He's delirious!... Do as you choose, but above all don't tell anyone we saw you."

He slung his rifle back over his shoulder and motioned to his son. The boy drew a candle and a box of matches out of his pocket.

"You'll get a meal every day and a clean blanket once a month. That's all we can do for you. The boy will bring them."

"I'll pretend I'm out squirrel hunting," said Etienne, "to divert the Jerries' attention. Good night, and you needn't worry, there aren't any wolves in this part of the woods."

"I must have strangled the last one last night," answered the man, tilting the candle toward his bloody hand.

Etienne understood instinctively that when he brought the meal the following day, he should bring a dagger as well. A rifle would alert the Germans. That was the beginning of the amazing telepathy that would unite them for the three years he lived amongst us, and that probably still unites them today, the one in his grave in Colmar and the other standing among the ostriches, over there in the Australian outback.

Before that crazy Breton woman came and dragged him away from his homeland, Etienne told me that on stormy nights he sometimes heard him, and he didn't feel there was anything supernatural about it; it was simply the voice of one friend stirring up another friend's memories. It's true your uncle was the first man Etienne built a solid friendship with out here in this inhospitable, battle-stricken, wolf-infested forest.

The next day, and all the following days, they spent many hours together just looking at each other without saying anything, nibbling on crusts of bread. Since he refused to eat bacon and since cheese had to be used sparingly, his meals consisted mostly of bread, sometimes accompanied with cabbage soup or a bunch of radishes. Luckily Etienne knew every square inch of the Bois de Chenois; he would saunter off to catch a woodcock or trap a hare, then make a fire and roast his catch, allowing the man to feast on it before taking the leftovers back to the house.

One day, after setting the food down in front of the hut the black man had built for himself, Etienne suddenly had the feeling he'd been followed. He looked over his shoulder, squinted through the wildflowers, and was finally able to make out a figure wearing a gray raincoat. Just as he was motioning the fugitive to hide, he recognized his mother's voice.

"It's me, Etienne! Tell him not to fret!" She drew near and stuck her head into the hole that served as a doorway.

"I've found something better for you. This evening Etienne will come and lead you there. Here, I've brought you some cheese."

Young Etienne didn't understand immediately. He didn't see the light—the truth didn't dawn on him until that evening after dinner, when his mother crept quietly into his room and slipped something into his hands.

"Here, now you know what you need to do."

"The keys to the school! They'd been hanging near the skillets and pothooks for years, growing dull with smoke and dust without anyone ever remarking them. And for good reason! They were the keys to his mother's complimentary apartment, or, more precisely, the apartment she was entitled to as principal of the school.

Young Etienne's heart sank into a gloom that was never to leave him. His mother wanted him to go and get that man, a black man, the only one in town or anywhere near it, and lead him to that cramped apartment nestled up above the classrooms that she'd never wanted to occupy both because it was too small and because she'd inherited the family home in Petit-Bourg only a stone's throw from there. It was a true country house with a thatched roof, a chimney, and a stone laundry sink. She wanted him to do this unbeknownst to her husband, the Jerries, and the informers!

Dear God, he thought as he left the house, *now the true war will begin. It will break out in the kitchen and then make its way up to the attic.*

To avoid patrols, he followed muddy paths and effortlessly covered the few miles that led to that hut I mentioned earlier. As he walked, his mind was completely absorbed with thoughts of the storm that was beginning to darken and muster over his family nest, the storm that would break in the peaceful skies of his youth—nothing could stop it now.

His parents had met one another soon after the Great War, in which they had both been courageous volunteers, sacrificing their youthful dreams. She had just shed her ambulance driver's jacket; he had recently left the trenches, eyes weakened and lungs damaged by the gases. He was twenty years her elder. Despite that, they had never disagreed about anything—the color of the curtains, the virtues of education, or the benefits of secularism—and then along comes some black man from out of nowhere to rock the foundations of their peaceful household rooted in the very precepts of Vosgian traditions: family, hard work, *potaye* or mashed vegetables, and sheer boredom.

He was still thinking about that when he locked the door behind the fugitive after they'd walked for several hours to avoid German dogs and flashlights, making innumerable detours and long halts under the cover of the trees to catch their breath.

He slipped off his clogs because of the gravel in the courtyard, but it wasn't necessary. His father was waiting for him on the front porch.

"Where were you, Etienne?"

"Um, I was out watching the stars."

"There are no stars, Etienne—you can see that, boy."

Then he grumbled something, holding back a violent cough, before adding, "I hope you're not beginning to lose your mind, young man."

Later I'll tell you all about how he ended up here, how—in no time—he became one of the villagers of Romaincourt, how he was almost killed riding a bicycle, how he conquered the hearts of young women before anyone even knew his name. Nothing was of any importance back in those days and least of all the family name of strangers who were just passing through. We called him "the Negro" when he wasn't around and simply "Sir" to his face. It was convenient, practical, and it suited everyone fine. It didn't seem to bother him. A black man in our midst: it never even occurred to us to find it odd.

People didn't take notice of him because he had frizzy hair, or because he'd materialized out of a bitter winter night, but because he insisted on wearing his fez, his greatcoat, his Tirailleur belts, and maybe also because of that impenetrable gaze, the long silences that nothing could draw him out of.

Little by little, over years and years, the way a photograph gradually develops, he has slowly emerged from the cloud of mystery to stand out very clearly. Only now am I able to truly see him, sixty years after his death. I can at long last make out his physical features and accurately take stock of his character traits.

Just like young Etienne, like the mayor, like the priest, like the roof of the church, like those *cheûlard*-boozers at Chez Marie, I'd never seen a black man before, and I first saw him from the back, Mister. From the back and very early in the morning, in the midst of the hubbub we would later learn had been caused by a munitions depot that had just been blown up in Vittel.

France had ceased being a republic and had become simply a small, ordinary, and secretive place. And since everyone lived under camouflage, I thought he'd disguised himself to escape the demons that haunted the burning cities and the roads of exodus. Sixty years later I still cringe in shame recalling what I said to Mama that evening when he came to the house for the first time.

"He's been traipsing around our streets for a month now. He should take off that mask of his now."

Mama made as if to give me a good wallop, Papa simply blushed, and Nonon Totor, who was always cracking up—even in the middle of mass—almost choked on his nip of plum brandy.

"Hee-hee, you little ninny, that's no mask, that's the way they come into this world. And he left his scar marks behind at that. Half the village would have run off if not, hee-hee!"

All of that took place when he'd already gone back out (headed over to Mâmiche Léontine's or maybe to the Colonel's), leaving us in the kitchen, where he'd discreetly set down his bundle of laundry.

God, how would he have reacted if he'd heard all that? Would he have shouted, drawn his revolver, or simply changed the subject, as he did later out on the church steps when Nonon Totor tried to get a smile out of him in front of a bunch of onlookers? I still wonder today how those two could have gotten along so well that they formed the most improbable pair ever seen in Romaincourt: one a proud Muslim, a very reserved, elegant African, and the other a good old Vosgian devoted to pork sausage, moonshine, line fishing, and coarse jokes.

I don't mean to brag, but I was closer to him than anyone. I roasted chestnuts for him, prepared his hot-water bottle, washed his clothes—except for his socks—but that's yet another story...

Young Etienne found him, that cocky Pinéguette girl thought of herself as his daughter, but I knew him better than anyone. For instance, see that package over there by the radio? I prepared it just for you. When it's time to get back on the airplane, take it with you and show it to your tribe proudly. Let them know he hasn't been forgotten. And while you're at it, I don't suppose you'll forget to remind them what the witch doctor said, "Your son is a hero, he won't be forgotten, Peuhl! Let us sing! To sing the courage of the dead is to dry the tears of the living!" In that package you'll find his uniform, his photographs, the correspondence, his Koran.

When the Jerries wounded him and everyone was busy watching how much fun those bastards were having dragging him around on the ground before they threw him into the patrol wagon without even putting so much as a bandage on him, I slipped into his room to collect his possessions. I knew they'd come to search the place, and since no one would have thought that a kid my age could come up with an idea like that, I wrapped them in plastic and buried them till the end of the war.

He and I didn't become friends immediately, quite the contrary. Our first encounters were more than difficult. He was too composed, too overbearing, too sure of himself, and I, just a little brat of a girl who, aside from her mama and papa, answered to no one but God himself.

I was seventeen years old, and I'd been taught to be wary of everything: wolves, bears, and most of all men, especially Rapennes and black men. However, my parents had opened their door to that particular one without giving it much thought. Papa, who was sparing with words, let him listen to the radio while sipping a cup of *aouatte* or watery chicory, and Mama, who was an expert cook, always served him some of her best dishes, like cabbage soup or a hearty raclette on days when we had cow's cheese or *géromé*, as we call it.

To be honest, he didn't take much interest in me at the time. It was near the end of his life that we truly got to know each other—a year before they shot him—back when I took part in the Resistance without realizing it. In the beginning, he'd mostly talk with Mama and Papa or else he'd chat with Mâmiche Léontine, who was always trying to find out more about him without much success. As far as I was concerned, he would never address me directly, choosing instead to talk to my parents in that African big brother tone of voice that infuriated me. "Mr. Tergoresse, don't you believe that Germaine should wait a little longer before wearing earrings... ? If I were you, Mrs. Tergoresse, I would marry my daughter right away. If not, she's likely to get into trouble, and this idea of sending her off to Nancy to continue her secondary studies is simply ill-founded."

My parents were all ears and that made me seethe. As if he were a nephew, an uncle, even our family's founding father. He'd ended up becoming a Tergoresse, without my even realizing it. Him, a Tergoresse! How absurd.

He only spent three years with us, but Mama said she felt as if he'd always been here, without our knowing it, a bit like those clouds that form right before your eyes and you wonder where they might have come from.

Now that our duty of remembrance has been done, now that his destiny has been fulfilled, I think what she said was true. That man was already here before I came into the world, caught up in the sunlight, in the vibrations in the air, in the rustling sounds of the night, and then—one fine day—something was triggered and he appeared before our eyes, mingled in with our lives, and in the end he became a star that will forever shine in the Romaincourt sky.

Now, no matter what I do, he remains standing—upright and irrefutable—in a corner of my mind. And it flatters me to know that it was him, the little man I lived next door to when I was seventeen, the man I'd seen playing checkers, tracing arabesques, or wolfing down his *frichti*—or grub—so many times. There was nothing ordinary about his life; it's rather as if he died twice and was buried three times. And now it's all become official, due to that lovely plaque shining out over there on the walls he used to live within; due to your having come here, the receptions that have been held in your honor, in our town and in Epinal, and the medals that you've been presented with. I just want you to know one thing, Mister, your uncle is not a hero—he's much more than that. Heroes can be found in granite and bronze. Let them cut their ribbons and bring on their fanfares! To me, he is first and foremost the friend or the father almost everyone would have liked to have had.

That, of course, was something that cocky Pinéguette girl just couldn't fathom. There had never been any heroes here; we got by quite well without them until people came over here making us feel guilty with those exhausting meetings and those incomprehensible slogans. We knew he died for us—we knew that! But to give him a street in the village! No, no, the people who'd known him contented themselves with describing his military appearance and his exploits with women or, like good old Celestin, pinning his photograph up over his pillow, or even (before diabetes confined him to his bed) making a silent march to Mount Virgin on the anniversary of his death. Dedicating a street to him had never crossed our minds. For that matter, we didn't even know that streets could be called Pierre or Jacques. Here, ours are called Church Street, School Street, White Pear Street, at least up until this morning, since from now on the main street is named after him.

But before getting to that point, he was at first that strange creature seen half-dead under the whitebeam bushes.

Did you know, Mister, that weeks after he'd been found, he still hadn't said anything about his name, his origins, his serial number, not one word?

I wasn't aware he'd been on a three-month expedition before reaching here. Three months to get from Saint-André-les-Vosges to Romaincourt! I had no idea it took so long to cover five kilometers! I was at the age when you don't need to know much of anything. Take, for example, the village of Saint-André-les-Vosges: I'd never set foot there, was content just to gaze at its silo and the church steeple from up on Sapinière Ridge.

As for young Etienne, I might have seen him once or twice trotting around with a bunch of other kids who would pass through here heading up to the hilltops to gather chestnuts. I wouldn't really meet him until the Saint Bartholomew Pig Feast. But he's never stopped writing me since then, sometimes more than ten postcards a year. My son wouldn't have done better if I'd had a son. Etienne is truly a boy from our parts. In Peru or at the North Pole, his thoughts will always be turned toward this place, the gripping cold around here, the howling wind, the tousled beech trees, the reserved, touchy folk of this region. He knows this land inside out—it saw him come into the world; an invisible bond ties him to each of its stones, each of its churches, each of its streets.

He never had any trouble with anyone, not even the *cheûlard*-boozers from Chez Marie, not even the priest who suspected everyone of being an irredeemable pagan, not even the Rapennes (not even Cyprien despite the... but that's an old story I'm not supposed to tell you about, a story I certainly won't tell you about for that matter).

I just want you to know that time has changed nothing, Etienne is still tied to us all, and we're tied to him, the living as well as the dead—especially the dead. He always asks me to put flowers on the graves on All Saints' Day, and I can tell by the way the wind blows afterward that the dead are quite pleased he thought of them. He's still tied to me too; he sends me wool, wooden statues, as well as the postcards. The didjeridoo hanging over there on the wall came from him too. A long time ago, he used to give me something altogether different, but there's no use in talking about that—what good does it do to dig up things that have been buried with the years? He doesn't come back very often, but on the rare occasions he does, everyone talks to everyone else whereas no one has talked to anyone for going on sixty years now. We drink brandy and devour smoked *fuseau* sausage. Sometimes we bring out the champagne and it's like a party. Everyone is always happy to see Etienne again.

You can't say as much for the Pinéguette girl. Pinéguette also went away, but she went on the journey you never come back from, Mister. Ah, that girl, no need to utter her name, simply say the Pinéguette girl, and the whole country will spit on the ground and then turn their back on you. But it's not right to speak of the dead in that way. Mâmiche Léontine would certainly scold me if she could hear me. Oh, sweet Jesus, please accept this sign of the cross and forgive that poor soul even though she never forgave anyone for anything!

I don't suppose that the Saint Bartholomew Pig Feast means anything to you. We usually celebrate Saint Nicholas, the patron saint of the Vosges. But that particular year it was secretly decided we would kill as many pigs as possible to keep them from ending up in the Germans' stew pots. The neighboring towns joined us, and we all ate blood sausage and sang "La Marseillaise" in private. A wonderful evening, Mister! Tergoresses and Rapennes spoke to each other on that night as they hadn't done in decades. I remember it was snowing and Etienne was there with his mother. And your uncle took our hands and did his big brother act. "Come along, you two young people! My word, you were made to get along with one another. When you've finished growing up, Germaine, I'll suggest that this young man become your fiancé."

He knew what he was saying: he was the only one in the whole village who could still stand up straight, his loathing for alcohol was second only to that which he felt for the Germans. As for me, a few glasses of plum brandy had been enough to make me feel merry, nevertheless I do remember the words I shot back at him, "A fiancé? But, my handsome Tirailleur, I should propose one for you if you didn't already have so many," and I immediately drew him into the circle of dancers to prevent him from exploding in an angry reprimand. "I'll straighten you out, Germaine, mark my words, I'll straighten you out!" I held him very close to my breast and burst out laughing in that shameless young girl laughter that made him furious. Our relationship was always marked with a certain distance, a certain respect, punctuated with mischievous teasing—and I was the one who wanted it that way.

It irritated me to see that foreigner from the colonies impose his authority so easily. My parents, the mayor, the Colonel, all bowed down before that bit of a soft-voiced man, who didn't even need to lift a finger to be obeyed. Everyone but the priest! The priest would have always been wary of him because he was black and didn't act like everyone else. Because being a Muslim, he didn't eat pork or drink moonshine, because he was always nosing around everywhere, meddling in everything, back in the days when a simple sneeze was enough to turn the world upside down. Because the priest had a thousand other reasons to avoid him, to show him he had no need of him.

It was a situation your uncle found terribly amusing. When they would run into one another, he'd stand at attention.

"Good day to you, dear Reverend Father!"

"Good day, my good black man!"

Then, satisfied with his number, he'd watch the man in the cassock walking away grumbling to ease his ill humor.

"I know you're making fun of me. But just wait, next time I won't even answer... Sweet Jesus, why didn't you make two different main streets running through this blasted village?"

I was the only one who dared stand up to him, and I'm darn proud of it. We were immediately "at odds" as soon as he came into this house for his first meal.

"You'll wash my socks!" he said after having rinsed his mouth. That was a quirk of his, rinsing his mouth every time he ate something.

"Never! I will never wash your socks! I'd rather die!"

Papa was doubled up laughing whereas Mama, shocked by the words she'd just heard, let a glass or a cup slip out of her hands, ashamed that her daughter dared speak to the honorable Tirailleur in such a way.

"I'll straighten your daughter out, upon my word, Mr. Tergoresse, I'll straighten her out!" he said as he made for the door. He spat in fury and jumped on his bicycle, and his voice boomed out through the village as he went clanking down the steep slope of the main street on his rattletrap sounding like a broken-down cart.

"I'll straighten her out, Mr. Tergoresse!"

That's the one image I'll always have of him, a small little man in a Tirailleur uniform astride his bike hurdling down the slopes of the Vosges as if he were going to war. However, one does not hurdle down the slopes of the Vosges like greased lightning on a cycle from before the First World War in total impunity.

"Rest assured, you'll break your neck one of these days, believe me."

"Mind your own business, Germaine!" he responded.

"You can't say I didn't warn you."

One morning when his first year in Romaincourt was coming to an end, what was bound to happen happened. He brought his laundry over, ate his quiche, and jumped on what he, with a sort of boyish mischievousness, used to call his "trusty steed." I stood up on the porch to watch him show off. And suddenly I was seeing the scene I had imagined over and over again in my mind actually happen. The contraption skidded on a patch of ice, slammed into the low wall of the washhouse, flipped over eight times, landing over by the water tank while he continued sliding down toward the war memorial.

"There you go," I said, splitting my sides laughing. "I told you so, didn't I? I told you so!"

Mama came running out of the garden and, for the first time in her life, slapped me in the face as she went past before joining the gathering that had quickly formed around him.

"Shut up, you little idiot, just shut up!"

And Mâmiche Léontine leapt out of her house, letting her basket of potatoes fall to the ground.

"*Oye, oye! Môn! Il s'est chié, le sergent, oyé, quelle chale avvaire*! Aiee, aiee! Lord! The Sergeant's gone and killed himself! What a disaster!"

The mayor went running away from the body sprawled out in the snow, disappeared into his house for an instant, then came back out with a stretcher, and I had never been so ashamed in my life. The village of Romaincourt in tears carried his bloody body up to the porch where we stood. We cleaned his wounds with the garden hose and then laid him out in the parlor to apply bandages and Mercurochrome.

"It certainly would top all if someone who survived the Battle of the Meuse succumbed to a fall from a bicycle in a Romaincourt street!" giggled my uncle Totor, who had never understood anything about the gravity of existence.

"Shut up, you loaf, or I'll lay you flat!" shouted the mayor as he cut gauze compresses.

"See what folks who bear the Tergoresse name are like?" said Cyprien Rapenne, who never missed an opportunity to revive the feud.

"Shut up all of you and run to Lamarche to call the firemen!" grumbled my aunt Marie.

While we'd thought him dead or unconscious, he moved on the stretcher and motioned *no* with his finger. The mayor turned toward his wife.

"Marie, dear, you've got to admit he's absolutely right. The firemen would mean the hospital in Epinal, investigations, the Jerries, and all the rest. We must keep this to ourselves. He'll recover quickly, you'll see—these black people are robust, even when they aren't."

We fixed up a room for him in our house, and the task of caring for him until his thigh healed up fell to me. I'd bring him a cup of chamomile tea and read him Péguy's *Notre Jeunesse* and Alfred de Vigny's *Death of the Wolf*, the only texts he put any store in because they were the only ones that counted in the eyes of Yolande Valdenaire, who had become his "mother" in the meantime. She'd struck back up with him as soon as the rumor of his presence here started going around.

"Would you like for me to wash your socks?"

"It's much too late for that, my little Germaine, much too late."

"I don't mind, I really don't."

"Then you should have made up your mind earlier."

He knew perfectly well what I was up to, what with his African craftiness and his military pride. But do you think he would help me make amends? For him, a mistake was a mistake; I'd made fun of him when he was on the verge of death, I had to pay for it as long as I lived. Never again were socks mentioned between us after that. And yet, from that day onward, Mama no longer washed them for him, I did—but he never learned of it.

That accident stood out as a milestone for us. We'd say "the year of the accident" just as we would "the year of the Saint Bartholomew Pig Feast." From then on, for him as well as for the rest of the village, there was the life that had preceded it and a different one afterward. It was our reference point, our year zero.

What he was and what he had done before then—I mean before coming to our village—will always remain in the realm of legend, chock-full of implausible details, scattered with windy paths and gray areas. But Etienne's account has helped make things seem more concrete, clearer, somewhat coherent.

It's a well-known fact that he first appeared at the edge of the Bois de Chenois, wounded and starving, looking more like a hunted animal than a human creature. That in spite of Yolande's husband being very reticent, she succeeded in hiding him in Saint-André-les-Vosges. Where? In a room above the classroom of the public school, right in the middle of the village! I can picture him in there, all huddled up to keep from dying of cold, waiting for his daily pot of soup, having to remain still, not cough, not sneeze, not knock against the wooden floor or make the cot squeak.

And then in November, that incident about food supplies broke out in La Rouille, when some crackpot farmers dared to protest about the excessive measures taken by the Feldkommandantur. Hundreds of Jerries went swarming over the area with their dogs and their tanks. And just guess where they set up camp? In Saint-André-les-Vosges! Near the fountain, Mister! Only two hundred yards from the school and right on the corner of the road leading to Petit-Bourg. They stayed there for five days, Mister. One won't die of hunger in five days, but one will die of thirst, unless he's a dromedary. He knew that perfectly well since he'd wandered about for weeks and weeks in all the forests of the Vosges before the Valdenaires found him half-dead in a wild boar's furrow.

One night, no longer able to bear it, he slipped out of the room, crept stealthily down the stairs, leapt over the wire fence, and landed as nimbly as a cat beside the street. A dog barked. The beam of a projector swept over the entire area around the fountain. Nervous, muffled voices in cavernous German accents tore through the night.

He thought they'd come for him. Cooped up in the tiny cubicle, he had no idea of what was going on outside: neither the peasant revolt nor the inexplicable presence of tanks and dogs. Lying flat on the ground, he was able to slither over to an elderberry bush overhanging the wire fence and hide there—its roots smelled strongly of piss. But he knew the dogs had already scented him, were preparing to lunge forward. *This time,* he thought, *I won't be able to escape them. Either they execute me immediately and the whole ordeal will be over with, or they take me pris-*

oner and I'll try to break out a second time. Lost in these thoughts, he didn't notice two Germans with two leashed dogs that were almost as tall as he was.

"Ein Neger! Ein Neger!"

He found himself dangling in the air, two colossal and cruel hands clamped over each of his ears.

" *Scheisse Neger, komm hier*! Shitty nigger, come over here!"

"Let me drink first!"

His guardian angels had only some twenty steps to take before dumping their burden at the foot of the tanks gathered around the fountain, and then they rained blows upon him while the dogs lunged, panting and gnashing. His empty stomach started growling, there was a taste of blood in his mouth, and he felt an acrid burn in his esophagus. He sank into unconsciousness, and then, once again, the odor of mud, the cold air, the brutish voices of his German jailers faded back in. He realized they were discussing his fate, and that filled him with hope. The only thing that counts in such circumstances is gaining time. Every fraction of a second multiplies by ten your chances of surviving or taking the advantage. Whoever happens to win that particular fraction, will win the war.

Later he found himself on a straw litter, probably in a prison, probably near a train station, since he could hear the shouts of the railway men and the sounds of the locomotives and boxcars. Were they going to transfer him? Torture him here before executing him? Push him in front of a locomotive? Those kinds of thoughts were running through his mind, creating even more intense pain than that which was burning his fingers and lips. He tried to estimate the time that had passed since he'd jumped over the wire fence of the school, but his mind grew blurry and he sank into unconsciousness again.

When he came to, he heard the jangling of keys through the door. He lifted himself painfully up on his elbow, prepared to reiterate his request.

"A little water, please!

But the man answered him in perfect French.

"Here you go."

He held out a chipped goblet and a little piece of black bread, closed the door, and leaned lazily against it.

"You're quite a lucky little man. The reason I'm saying that is because you had a close call yesterday. However, that doesn't mean you'll make it through today."

The man took off his kepi for a moment and scratched his head.

"You see, Mr. Senegalese Tirailleur, if I say you're lucky, it's because by pure chance you happened upon the Feldkommandantur. On the other side, only three hundred yards from the tree where they found you, the Gestapo would have picked you up. When the Feldkommandantur runs into guys like you and doesn't really know what to do with them, they entrust them to us. Whereas the Gestapo..."

"Do you mean to say that the French gendarmerie imprisons French soldiers for the Germans?"

"Don't make me regret having offered you food and water!"

"What do you intend to do with me?"

"Nothing. I have orders to leave you in Epinal, and it will be up to them to decide. It might be the firing squad; it might be the Second Company of the War Booty Battalion.

"What in the heck is that?"

"It's something they've come up with to deal with war booty. It's mostly made up of Africans, Malagasies, and Indochinese."

"So what do you do in this, whatever you call it? Gather, sort, and clean the rifles they've taken from us?"

"Exactly. And don't go telling me it's a pity, it's humiliating, or God knows what else. For me, that's just the way things are: it's the sit-u-a-tion! I don't want anyone crying on my shoulder. I hold French soldiers prisoner for the Germans, so what? France should either have won the war, or else gone to hell!"

He flew out of the room, screwing his kepi down on his head and slamming the door violently.

But he came back a few hours later just as the autumn evening was setting in. He brought a stool along with him that he set down in a corner of the room. Before taking his seat, he took out a packet of Gitanes cigarettes.

"Do you smoke?"

"No!"

"Fine, that's too bad! There's nothing more that I can do for you. You won't get any more bread and water until tomorrow—if they let you live till then."

He lit up his cigarette and blew perfect smoke rings up to the ceiling.

"One of our friends in gendarmerie school used to be so good at it, you'd have thought they were slices of ham.... Obviously, you don't know how to do it... since you don't smoke.... What colony?"

"Guinea! French Guinea!"

"Do you know why I haven't asked you your name? Because you've all got the same name over there, and it's always downright impossible to pronounce to boot!"

He raised his head and closed his eyes for a long moment.

"Can I trust you?"

"At this point, I sincerely wonder what difference that makes."

"It's going to take place this evening. You won't be alone. Jews, communists, farmers, even German deserters. The truck leaves here at 20:06 hours and is scheduled to arrive at the barracks in Epinal at exactly 21:37 hours. You bet! That's why the Germans defeated us: they respect the hierarchy and punctuality religiously.... Now, listen to me! At 20:22 hours we'll be at the railway crossing. That's when the train from Nancy to Langres goes by. The crossing gates will stay down for three minutes, and the forest is less than five hundred yards from there.... There you have it! It's up to you to decide! We'll be shooting real bullets since we'll have to shoot. The German observation post is located on Mont des Fourches just above the railroad tracks. And Mont des Fourches, my friend, has eyes sharper than those of a jeweler. Three minutes, not a second more."

"Three minutes is almost an eternity at a time like that."

"I won't wish you good luck!"

"I wouldn't ask for so much... Chief Brigadier?"

"Thouvenet, Julien Thouvenet!"

"I'll remember that name, even when they've filled my belly with lead."

In all, seven of them attempted to make a run for it. Four were shot down. Three made it into the forest. In spite of that, he still didn't feel he was out of danger, even three days afterward. He still knew nothing about this country, its *ballons* or rounded mountain tops, its legends, nothing about its family secrets, but he'd learned to partake of its berries, its wild bulbs, the tangy water of its ponds and washes. He'd grown used to the biting icy air that rips into your lungs with the slightest breath. He'd grown used to the wild smell of its woods, to its harsh nights filled with the howling of the wind and the wolves.

It was simple: you had to lie low during the day, only come out after dusk, force yourself to sleep in spite of the brutal cold, dress your wounds with whatever was at hand—black mud, snail's slime, fern sap. A compass would have been of no use. To the south or the east, he would have come up against the same inevitable dangers: hunger, solitude, cold, and the constant risk of being shot down or turned in. How long did he wander around like that, staggering, half bent over, legs burning up, face lashed by the stalks of wild onions and leeks until he landed in that cabin over by Romain-aux-Bois that I showed you yesterday; the one where his kettle and hatchet still remain? For weeks probably, prowling around the livestock, running up against fences and closed doors, the wary and hostile faces of poachers and honey hunters!

It was a hunter's cabin where the forest ranger usually left his gear. Luckily there was a stove, and on the rough-hewn wooden shelf, a sack of coal next to the pot and the stove door. But since he had no means of lighting a fire, since he was no longer hot nor cold, nor hungry, but just totally dazed, and it felt as if the life were draining from his body....

He collapsed in a corner of the room, allowed himself to be submerged in the slow, salutary wave of unconsciousness. It was not until the next day that he noticed a small metal frame bed in the opposite corner of the room, with a mattress, a pillow, and even a thick mountain quilt in fairly good shape. Although he was evidently famished and feeble the next day, he was inhabited by a furious will to get to his feet, struggle, either be victorious or die, and a small glimmer of joy was even kindling in his heart again.

Gripping a knife, he dragged himself in the direction of the nearest village, guided by the smell of bread and the sound of dogs. He crouched behind the first house he came upon and observed. Nothing, nothing was happening. Perhaps they were all dead or had been deported, but there was the sound of the dogs and that maddening smell of bread. He moved down the main street, taking cover first behind a nearby tree, then darting behind a wall farther along, as he'd been taught to do in the army.

Sounds. A door squeaking. Bursts of laughter.

A figure came out, pissed noisily on the gardenias lining the sidewalk, and teetered down to the other end of the street singing a bawdy song in a hoarse voice. He waited for him to turn the corner before drawing closer. He put his nose up to the window: it was a combination bar-bakery, with shabby furniture and a wooden counter. There were approximately ten dreary-looking patrons inside—one was an old man with a white beard wearing a cap—all were sipping silently at the liquor served them by a young woman whose features were already hardened by work in the fields. No one paid any attention to him, and none of them seemed to be armed.

He put his hand on his right pocket where the knife lay and pushed the heavy oak door open with his elbow. They merely turned their heads toward him, without moving, without showing any sign of surprise or fright. The strange scene, in which the world seemed to have come to a sudden halt, dragged out for one or two minutes, then the young woman, standing tall in her clogs, sashayed over to him swaying her hips in her old gray dress.

"Oh, look! A black man! Come along now, don't just stand there like that," she scolded.

She closed the door to keep out the wind and the snowflakes that were swirling into the room, plastering themselves against the stony, tired faces, against the edge of the counter. She took his hand gently and pulled him over to the table closest to the coal stove.

"Sit down here. I know just what you need."

The old man with the cap grimaced in disgust, spat on the floor, and took out a coin that he threw at the proprietress as he went out, slamming the door without saying good-bye. Two or three others followed him.

"Don't bother about them. The real men from around here are either dead or have been deported. All that's left are the cripples and the cowards."

She set a large steaming bowl down in front of him.

"Here, it's lentil soup with lots of bacon and pork rind."

This time he didn't have the strength to act like a purist. He emptied the bowl as the proprietress looked on compassionately, telling himself Allah would consider that he'd swallowed those couple of pieces of pork under extenuating circumstances. Afterward, he was given a bowl of chicory and a piece of cheese, then two apples and a cluster of gooseberries. He rinsed his mouth and went outside to spit.

"I have to go now," he said.

"Yes, it's best you go, it's best for us too."

She held out a round loaf of black bread and went on, "Go ahead, go out the back door."

"Give me a few embers in a crock."

"In this snow?"

She disappeared into the kitchen for a moment and came back with a piece of phosphorous and some matches.

"But where will you keep them? You're drenched."

She went back into the kitchen and came back with a candy tin.

"All right now, get on your way and take care!"

He found the wooden cabin again and hurried to light the coal stove. For the first time since the beginning of the war, he had a real home, a place all to himself—that is, if you don't count the rats, the fleas, and the wayward stags that would kick at the door during the night.

A kettle was lying under the metal bed and, in addition to a rifle and cartridges, the forest ranger's crate contained all the necessary equipment for fishing and trapping game.

Except, what good was a hunting rifle at that particular time in history? The Germans, who incidentally had confiscated them all, were alert to the slightest shot as were their French subordinates, who were anxious to avoid any trouble. And since he didn't know how to fish or trap game...

The heat was a welcome change, but, apart from that, he was still in the same predicament. He staved off hunger as best he could: berries, boiled leeks... When he could no longer bear the hunger, he crept over to the edge of the village to pick some apples or pull up a few bunches of carrots.

That lasted a week or two, then one day he heard someone knock at the door. He peered through the door frame and recognized the woman from the bar. Opening the door, he saw she wasn't alone. A boy of around eight years of age—probably her son—was standing next to her, trembling like a leaf.

"Uh... We don't mean to disturb you."

"Come in, Madame, it's much warmer inside.... Thanks to you...."

"Call me Huguette.... This is my son, Celestin! Here, we've brought you some food. It will help you get through for a few days."

She looked around the cabin, glanced disgustedly at the door obstructed with snow.

"You don't intend to stay here, do you?"

"Where do you want me to go?"

"You've got a point there!"

He rummaged through the bag and drew out a piece of bread, some cheese, chestnuts, ham, smoked herring, then his face lit up.

"Oh, chocolate! I haven't had any since I left Langeais."

"Langeais?"

"Are you familiar with Langeais?"

"I've heard of it. My mother was born in Vendôme. What were you doing in Langeais?"

"Nothing in particular, I just happened to grow up there."

"Well, I'll be—you grew up in Langeais?"

She whispered something to her son and dug around in the pocket of her coat that she hadn't taken off in spite of the heat the stove was giving off.

"I also brought you some cigarettes, but I presume you don't smoke?"

"And you do?"

"No! They're not really mine, they're my husband's."

"And where is your husband?"

She merely glanced at her watch.

"It's time to go. If we're able to get our hands on anything, Celestin will bring it to you. It's not easy, believe me—the Germans take eight out of every ten eggs laid. The same goes for milk, wood, wheat, pigs, and cows. They serve themselves first and leave the crumbs to the French. How do you expect a farmer to think of others when he hasn't got enough to eat himself?"

"But, your husband?"

"Perhaps we'll have a chance to talk about him. I'll be back. It's best if I come here. Back in town, tongues are beginning to wag."

"It will be a pleasure to see you again."

"That is if you haven't left in the meantime."

"Where in God's name could I go?"

"Switzerland isn't far from here. From there, you could make it to the free zone and then to Africa. You'd be nice and warm over there."

Once again, she darted a glum look outside. "This place isn't even fit for horned creatures, let alone human beings."

"How far are we from Chaumont?"

"Chaumont? What a strange thing to bring up!"

The following week, the Celestin boy brought milk, then eggs, then bread, then gooseberry jam. He'd walk up to the cabin, kick his clogs noisily on the woodpile stacked against the wall, then he'd knock, come in for a few minutes to set down the provisions and warm his hands. Finally, with his eyes bulging out of their sockets in fear of God only knows what, he'd rush out without saying good-bye and run away as fast as he could, sobbing. He'd never say anything about himself or about the weather or even about his mother.

His mother! She'd promised to come back, but she hadn't. In that wood cabin where life was almost back to normal again, with mornings and evenings, almost perfect heating, and food once or twice a day, lustful longings began to creep into his mind. He recalled that it had been exactly one year and two months since he'd touched a woman. Suddenly a feeling of intense yearning shot through him at the thought of the boy's mother who hadn't come.

A few days later, he was surprised to see her standing at the door in lieu of her faint-hearted son, and he was seized with an animal-like desire.

"Oh, it's you?" he said, swallowing his saliva with difficulty.

"I've only got a few turnips and a little cabbage. It's gotten to be unbearable, un-bear-a-ble!"

"I thought I'd never see you again!"

"The bar, the kid, the cooking, the housework! And also, people around here are talking, you know!"

He took hold of her arm and pinned her brusquely against the bed.

"Ow! You're hurting me!"

"Tell me about your husband!"

"Why do you want to know?"

"You promised you'd tell me!"

She managed to get loose and run over to sit by the coal stove.

"So, where is he?"

"He went away."

"With someone else?"

"Oh, that would have been so much better!"

He went over to dry her tears and lead her over to the bed more gently this time. Then she managed to suppress two or three heaving sobs and, snuggling up against him, told the story.

It was on a Tuesday last June, just after Armistice Day. Firmin was behind the counter, and she was in the kitchen, fixing dinner. It was almost ten o'clock in the evening. They should have closed up long before, but Firmin had kept a group of friends over drinking moonshine and sharing in his favorite pastime, berating the Jerries. You'd have thought that everything had been put purposefully in to place for that night to end in tragedy. Good old Firmin was drunk, drunker than usual, and his friends were just as drunk. They were bawling out rousing barroom songs and rivaling one another with sinister jokes about the Jerries.

"You know how Germans go about screwing? Well, they..."

And just when he was about to finish his sentence, a Gestapo platoon came marching past the bar in the direction of Roncourt.

"Look, those dogs come right when they're called! There they are the bastards!"

He took out a French flag and started singing "La Marseillaise" at the top of his lungs. But he was the only one who dared do so, which was why he was the only one who was picked up. They tortured him in Epinal and then threw him on the first train bound for Germany.

"Not a scrap of news since then, Mister," she said, beginning to sob again. "Some people say he's in the Sonnenburg camp; others say it's the one in Sachsenhausen. That Firmin, he just couldn't miss a chance to sing 'La Marseillaise' in front of those bastards. He was an anarchist, you know."

He dried her cheeks gently, touched her lips with his. She did not move, did not push him away, did not respond to his advances either. He fondled her breasts and lifted her skirt.

"You know how long it's been since I knew a woman, Huguette?... Since the beginning of the war."

"That's more than a year!" she answered in a voice that was simply astonished, not frightened, not offended in the least.

"Do you think that's normal, Huguette?"

"Oh, no!"

"I want you, Huguette, and I'm not ashamed to say so. That shocks you though, doesn't it, Huguette?"

"No, no," she whimpered. "It's just that..."

"It's just that you don't love me, Huguette, isn't that right?"

"You just refuse to understand. You don't know what Dr. Couillaud told me: there's a baby growing in my belly, my husband's baby. They'll never see one another, Mister: this child will never know his father, I'm certain of it."

They remained clinging to one another for a long time rocked by their breathing and the almost audible sound of their confused thoughts. Then he stood up, helped her arrange her brassiere and skirt.

"Very well, in that case, Huguette, we'll act as if we were brother and sister!"

Her visits and those of her son grew to be few and far between, due to the Jerries, due to the fact that food was growing ever harder to find, scarcer by the day. Once again, he was forced to turn to the forest for food and drink, and gradually he began to forget her. But when he heard a knock at the door a few days later, he knew it was her and remarked to himself that it was the first time she'd come to visit him at night.

"Someone wants to see you," she told him as soon as she stepped inside.

He went out to peer into the dark night. Over by the woodpile, a human figure finally stood out against the pale reflections of snow. Evidently, the person wished to remain at a distance as if afraid of something or as if, on the contrary, he harbored some ill intention.

"I'm sorry about what happened to you!"

It was Yolande. It was no longer necessary to shine a flashlight on the enigmatic form, so indistinct, so shapeless that it seemed to be sculpted out of the very matter of night, that calm, even voice was more than enough for him to recognize her.

"Come in, both of you—you'll die of cold!"

He led them over to the stove and waited for them to warm themselves. He knew how hard it was to talk or think after a long walk in the snow-laden forest of the Vosges.

"She thought you were dead," said Huguette, taking some fried chicken and Gruyère cheese out of her old frayed shopping bag.

"As soon as you'd been taken away, they shot two hundred men in the Fouchécourt quarries. Two hundred, many of whom were Guineans! I was convinced you were among them. Then day before yesterday, a trapper talked to me about the black man in Romain-aux-Bois, and I told myself it had to be you."

"Come and have some of this chicken for me," said Huguette. "God knows whether there'll be any tomorrow."

He tore off a quarter of the bird and gulped it down without leaving the tiniest bone. He took a piece of paper from the pile of old newspapers he used for lighting the coal stove to wrap the rest in and stowed it away high on the shelf.

"Have some cheese too."

He didn't answer. He went and scooped up some snow that he melted in an old goblet to rinse out his mouth.

"It's such a pleasure to eat one's fill, but even a greater one to see the two of you alive and well, along with myself!"

"It's my fault. I should have thought to leave you enough water and food to get through the winter. No one would have imagined they'd stop with their tanks and equipment around the fountain for almost a week, as if they knew Etienne would walk right past there bringing you your soup."

"What happened that day?"

"A peasant uprising or something like that," explained Yolande. "I don't much appreciate Etienne's habit of running around in the woods in search of game, but I do admit that if it hadn't been for his poacher's instinct, we would have all been goners that day. As he was leaving Petit-Bourg, he heard the Gestapo's dogs and saw the officers, more nervous than usual, swarming over the hillsides. So he sniffed at the air and sensed that something shady was in the making. He thought about you, about your prison, about your empty stomach, but he preferred to be cautious and turn back. And it was the right thing to do, I assure you, because—God knows why—I'd been stupid enough to have given him a letter for you."

"And what did the letter say?"

Evidently embarrassed, she glanced first at Huguette, then at the stove, until she finally turned to face him.

"Well, we'll surely have a chance to talk about that."

She stood up before finishing her sentence, slowly took off her coat, and methodically unhooked the cloth bag she was carrying on her hips.

"Here, this is all I was able to do."

He didn't open it immediately to see what it contained, but feeling the shapes inside the bag, he guessed it was a sufficient quantity of sardines and canned food to last a week or two.

She put her coat back on and motioned to Huguette that it was time to leave. She glanced around at the walls and the roof made of poorly fitted logs that let in the rain and snow, the sun or the wind.

"It's better that you stay here. The school has become dangerous for you. People have started gossiping. My husband knows about it; the Jerries are suspicious. I'll try to come back, or else I'll send messages. Huguette and Celestin can be our relays."

"I spoke to him about Switzerland, but he's only got one thing on his mind: Chaumont."

"I know, my husband told me. We've all developed quirky obsessions since this war began."

The following days were among the happiest in his life as a black nomad: he had food and drink, he was warm, he'd seen Yolande again, the squirrels were rubbing up against the trunks of the trees around the cabin, and the birds were singing a gay tune. Yolande! Huguette! Dear God, how long had it been since he'd been with a woman?

Huguette or Yolande?

Yolande, he didn't yet call her "Mama." But she'd saved his life, and ever since they first met in the Bois de Chenois, he'd felt the imposing maternal authority of that elegant, austerely beautiful woman, and in spite of that—or because of it—she would continue to provoke strong and confused emotions in him all through the years of torment, right up until they were both crushed under wheels of the Gestapo.

As far as Huguette was concerned, that was over with—over with before it even began, the fault of the seed that was growing in her belly, and that, in itself, summed up the cruelty of the times. Woman is God's workshop, as the wise men from back in his land said. To touch a pregnant woman is to defile the house of Allah, interrupt the order of the Universe.

Huguette or Yolande, Yolande or Huguette? Why is it that forbidden women are always more desirable than others?

He let the days slip by without thinking about Guinea, without thinking about Langeais or about his friends and the women in Paris, without even thinking about the war. That's how the creatures all around him probably lived, happy to eat and sleep and not think about anything, especially not about war.

It wasn't until quite some time later that things grew to be so complicated, he ended up telling himself he might have been better off being killed in the Battle of the Meuse. Winter followed autumn and he still had one turnip, two leeks, a piece of Gruyère cheese, and five tins of sardines. Then he came up against something he'd never experienced in all his life in France, neither in Langeais, nor in Paris, nor in Sanary-sur-Mer, nor in La Rochelle—the Vosgian winter, with its furious winds, its three-foot-deep snow, its piles of frozen birds, and its nights that drew out for twenty hours or more.

Watching the daylight wane when it wasn't even three o'clock in the afternoon, he thought it must be a joke: everything would go back to normal in a minute, as soon as that swarm of crows or that cloud of gas undoubtedly released by those cursed Germans passed over. Except the next day, the mist was still there, just as silent and impenetrable as the day before, and it wasn't until ten o'clock in the morning that the first rays of sunlight were able to shine through. Soon, the old cart disappeared, engulfed in snow, and the water tank collapsed. Soon, he became aware that he could no longer open the door without giving it a strong shove with his shoulder and that he couldn't reach the woodpile until he removed ten shovelfuls of snow. He realized how serious the situation was when he began to be unable to feel his fingers anymore.

Everything around him had fallen silent. No more twittering of birds, no more sounds of squirrels against the tree trunks, no more braying of stags under the tall chestnut trees, no more human voices, no more sounds of horse-drawn carts coming from the road. He realized how easily one might go mad being alone in the world. He told himself that life is but a long chain of interlinking sounds, should a single one be withdrawn, existence itself would be undermined.

He was no longer living in a cabin, but in a prison to which he held the key; an island of rotten wood separated from the world by a vast ocean of snow. Neither Yolande nor Huguette nor Celestin would come back, nor would the rats, the mice, or the bugs. He stopped going out to stretch his legs because the wind would blow him over, and he was blinded by the harsh glare of the snow. But when the roof collapsed in the middle of the night and a single gust of wind buried the metal bed and the stove, he told himself it would be better to die elsewhere. Someplace where—though no one would shed a tear—someone might at least throw him into a hole. He cast away the now-useless matches, put the last tin of sardines in his pocket, and went out. Of course, he intended to make it as far as Romain-aux-Bois and knock at the door of the bar. Huguette would come and open up for him. She'd offer him a bowl of soup or some chicory, then he'd take her in his arms and listen to her cry and bask in her warmth, her tenderness, her smell. He'd learned how to orientate himself since the last time; he had to walk away leaving the horse cart to his left and the old water tank to his right, cross the pinewoods till he reached the abandoned farm, trot along for almost an hour till he got to the dairy farm, then he should look for the road on the right and follow it walking through the underbrush until he reached the first houses. Except there was no more horse cart, no more water tank, no more farm or pinewoods, no north, no south. The world was nothing but a huge field of glaring snow that burned your eyes. He didn't sight those first houses he'd wished so hard for until early morning. He hastened his pace but collapsed in front of the very first door. It was that idiot Cyprien Rapenne who found him as he was going out to milk his cow. He let out a cry and immediately ran to wake up the mayor.

"There's a nigger in Jondain Street."

"And what's he doing there?"

"Nothing, he's just dying, that's all."

That's how, upon awakening one fine morning, we learned that there was a Negro in our midst, Mister. A real Negro, as black as you can still find them over there in your forests in Africa. His cheeks were swollen and his feet were bloody. People stood in line to come and see him in the mayor's parlor where he'd been stretched out. And of course everyone had something to say. And some of the silliest things in the world were said. So silly that the mayor—a known socialist and freemason—blustered furiously.

"No, he isn't from a circus or a zoo or a Mississippi plantation. He's a Senegalese Tirailleur, a soldier in the French army, you dopes!"

From Guinea, the Congo, or Chad... To us, all Tirailleurs were Senegalese. As were all black men on the planet.

When the man was able to speak, meaning the next day or the day after, the mayor put his hand on his forehead and asked, "Where did you come from, poor fellow?"

"From Harréville-les-Chanteurs."

"My God!"

"That nigger's a liar, Mister Mayor," said Cyprien Rapenne, indignant. "No one could survive that in this weather."

What he meant to say was that it was in Harréville-les-Chanteurs that his ordeal had begun and not in Saint-André-les-Vosges or Romain-aux-Bois. But we didn't learn the details of his journey until after his death, when Pinéguette, Celestin, and that man who called himself Colonel Melun decided to give us history lessons. Up until then, we could track him from the Bois de Chenois to Saint-André-les-Vosges; from Saint-André-les-Vosges to the gendarmerie in Lamarche; from there to Romain-aux-Bois. He never talked about himself—how were we to know? And then, sixty years after his death, all these important professors showed up and talked our ears off with a bunch of brand-new words: Guinea, Bomboli, Pelli-Foulayabé, Langeais, Baumont, Harréville-les-Chanteurs—places no one had ever heard of before. We had to pay very close attention and be very patient to straighten out all that hodgepodge.

Let's start with Harréville-les-Chanteurs: if it hadn't been for that village in the Haute-Marne, nothing would have happened and you wouldn't have come from your distant land of Guinea just to listen to a shriveled-up old *crapie* of a woman like me. That's where he was taken prisoner, Mister, during the famous Battle of the Meuse. It was probably on June 18, 1940. Pinéguette felt that date was very important. The day before, Marshal Pétain had made his address to the nation, and that very same day, De Gaulle had done likewise. But the Tirailleurs weren't aware of that; no one had told them. They'd been told, "Keep fighting down to the very last man, and let not a single dirty dog of a German get through." And from the Ardennes to the Haute-Marne, they'd fought with all of the conviction and vehemence they're so well known for.

Two regiments were supposed to keep the enemy from crossing the Meuse, the Fourteenth Regiment de Tirailleurs Sénégalais (RTS) stationed at Bourmont and the Twelfth, stationed at Harréville-les-Chanteurs. As you can guess, your uncle was in the Twelfth Regiment. Their mission was to defend a bridge. Only their carbines weren't very efficient against the German artillery. They resisted all day and all night from the eighteenth to the nineteenth, but early in the morning, famished, abandoned by their white superiors, and without munitions, they had to beat a retreat. The luckiest ones were able to disappear into the neighboring forests; he took refuge in a freight car. They arrested him in that freight car and had him taken to Neufchâteau, where he was imprisoned in the Rebeval barracks with several of his companions. He spent the entire summer building camps and the following winter shoveling snow off the roads.

In those barracks there were thousands of Tirailleurs, with a only few hundred Germans: mostly young soldiers and officers who, after a long campaign from Belgium, had gone through Epernay and Reims, where they'd acquired copious supplies of fine wines and champagne. Every evening they partied in the old barracks they used as a mess hall. Your uncle took advantage of one of their sumptuous binges to escape along with forty of his companions. That's how, four months later, he ended up here, chilled to the bone and covered with blood; that's how he came into our lives and never went out. He obviously didn't know he was in Romaincourt—he believed he was in Romain-aux-Bois, somewhat like that poor old Christopher Columbus who thought he was already in the East Indies when he reached the Antilles.

We weren't to learn much about his life or that of his companion escapees up until the encounter with the Valdenaires. I imagine it was very similar to the life he led in Romain-aux-Bois.

Mister, do you know that in one month, out of the sixty thousand Tirailleurs sent to the front lines, twenty-nine thousand were taken prisoner by the Germans? The others were either dead or wandering the forests of France, tracked down by the occupying forces, and not always welcomed by the French. Certain farmers gave them bread, even medicine or blankets; others went and turned them into to the Feldkommandantur or the Gestapo. Those who'd read the colonial manuals armed themselves with rifles and, once they'd spotted small isolated groups, went out monkey hunting, as was the practice back then in the forests of the Congo.

But the real question, Mister, is this: Why—out of the forty who escaped from Rebeval—was he the only one to reach Romaincourt? Yes, that's what we asked ourselves for a long time, until Colonel Melun explained it to us. They didn't have a chance of surviving in a group. Even a lone black man in the Vosgian countryside was already at risk.... Imagine the perils fifty or a hundred of them would have faced! The Africans knew that and had given orders—as far as that was possible—to spread out. Thousands of Senegalese Tirailleurs wandering about the forests of France, prey to hunger, to the Germans and the wolves. Amongst them, your uncle's friends, his companions from Rebeval, and the others who'd deserted on the night of the eighteenth when they realized they had no other choice. All the men who were hunted down, who were hung, executed, banished—all of them, I say—haunted him while he was delirious with fever. It was at least a week before he regained consciousness and was able to sit up on the edge of the bed by himself and eat the bowl of soup Mama held out to him. And the names he mumbled as he lay near death still remain in my mind as if they'd just been etched there. Farara Dantillah, Boubacar Diallo, Moriba Doumbouya, Moussa Kondé, Fodé Soumah, Zana, Adama Diougal, Nouffé Koumbou. And especially, the most resonant, most moving, most unforgettable name of all because it was the one he raved about most often: Va Messié, Va Messié, Va Messié!

How in God's name did those foreign, perplexing, unpronounceable words become so familiar to me in so little time? For the first time in my life, I was witnessing the death of a man, and my adolescent mind had prepared itself to receive his last confession and testament—that must be it. Except back in those years, the fog was terribly thick and it took me some time, a very long time, to sort things out and link each of those names to their allotted destinies.

They probably decided to part ways in the vicinity of Bazoilles. I say that because the night before, sixty black soldiers were camping around a pond when they were surrounded by the Germans, who threw them into a barn and set fire to it. So that's when they determined to separate, each of them taking a different direction; each relying only upon himself, each taking the tenuous thread of his destiny in hand. They gathered up twigs of different lengths and drew lots, each one having to wait one hour after his predecessor's departure before choosing his route.

I can just picture the ritual ceremony they must have performed before turning their backs on one another (where you people come from, nothing is done without a gris-gris and a kola nut). I can picture the hardy embraces and the nonchalant laughter; no, soldiers don't cry—their tears come out of their skin, not their eyes. Before that, another parting had taken place with no embraces or kola nuts that time. It had taken place on that fateful band of land that is as dreary and glaucous as the Meuse it runs parallel to, that deadly corridor sandwiched between the bridge and the tracks where boxcars weary of hauling useless reinforcements came to a halt for all time—mowed down by enemy machine-gun fire.

It was a slaughter, Mister. A lot of men from Sudan, from Dahomey, from the Ivory Coast! A lot from Guinea, oh yes, a lot from Guinea!

Tomorrow I'll show you the cemetery in Harréville-les-Chanteurs, and you can read the names on the graves that will be familiar to you: Kamara Moussa, Farara Dantillah, Moussa Kondé, Mansa Diallo, Magaria Niger. Then we'll go to Bugnéville, where a plaque was put up in honor Fodé Soumah, shot down by the Germans as he walked beside his inseparable companion, Moriba Doumbouya. Moriba, who survived, fled into the woods, where he was able to stay alive until winter, thanks to a farmer who gave him milk when he came to care for his animals and fell trees. But, as you'll recall, that was a particularly severe winter and very soon poor Moriba also endured the same trials as your uncle did over in Romain-aux-Bois. The good farmer ceased manifesting himself. Starving, freezing to death, Moriba came out of the woods, walked across the village, and went to sit down by the War Memorial, where he waited calmly for the Germans to come and throw him in a barn and light fire to it.

We didn't know anything about that ghostly army. We had no idea that only a few yards from our villages those people were dying or going mad in these hostile lands, and all for a cause that had absolutely nothing to do with them. Many of us thought your uncle was the only one, just because we hadn't seen any others. It wasn't until long after the war that we learned the truth. And who do we have to thank for that?

She was a pest, that Pinéguette, but if it hadn't been for her—I've nothing to lose by admitting it now—none of what's going on around us right now would have happened. It's all because of that Pinéguette girl but also because of poor Celestin, who's been let down so often by life that he's come sort of unstrung. If it weren't for the darned diabetes, he'd have come and given you a hug and shown you his pistol, the one your uncle gave him. Celestin isn't as crazy as she was; he couldn't bear her impulsiveness or her communard stances. But he told himself, just as she did, that people should know about the things that happened here.

They both went to fetch that man, Colonel Melun, a veteran from Indochina who'd decided to spend his retirement making amends for what he called "the shameful wrongs done to the Tirailleurs." He used to say, "These craftsmen of war exist on the battlefield alone. Once the war is over, they are discarded like used Kleenexes, goddamned bloody hell! No one thinks of them afterward!" It had to come out, it had to be made known, because, "for God's sake, Germany isn't the only country that has things to hide!"

Back in the days of your uncle, Colonel Melun was still wearing short trousers, but soon after he learned the ropes in Dien Bien Phu and Kabylie. There were Tirailleurs over there too, just as there had already been in the trenches in 1914 and in the cuirassiers in the Battle of Wœrth in 1870. The Colonel had fought for many years alongside those intrepid Africans, who were used as cannon fodder. He had taken stock of their loyalty and courage. It sickened him to see them booted back to their respective wastelands each time with bleeding lungs and missing legs; dazed, underestimated, never receiving distinctions or being mentioned on war memorials and to top it all off, being only entitled to a pension ten times inferior to that of their white colleagues.

So he had made up his mind to gather documentation, alert the press, and lay siege to the ministries. He wrote an article five years ago in a Parisian newspaper in which he spoke of your uncle. Pinéguette read it and, being the pesky brat she was, climbed up on her high horse. Of course, she just couldn't pass up that double opportunity: to have everyone talking about her and be able to yak our ears off with her grandiloquent and incomprehensible causes. She hastily sent off a letter in which she of course made herself out to be his daughter, a cousin of yours of sorts, although she was already fifty-six years old and not a single frizzy hair or any other negroid feature had ever confirmed the claim. But out of tact, or simply neglect, Colonel Melun paid no attention to that fact. Happy to have someone take him seriously at last, he immediately responded and hurried to Romaincourt as soon as he was invited to do so.

I tell you, that was the most painful torture she ever put us through. She had him visit the house over there in front of us, the one where the mayor had put him up, the forest ranger's cabin in Romain-aux-Bois, the Boène farm, the small apartment above the school in Saint-André-les-Vosges, and all the places he used to go when he was alive, the places that were so ordinary at the time and that now have become as famous in our eyes as the Louvre or the Pantheon.

And that evening, Mister, she set up a platform between the washhouse and the war monument, just a few steps from the church, right at Vespers time, Mister, in order to shout insults into a megaphone before allowing Colonel Melun to speak. She'd gone from door to door that afternoon forcing everyone to come and listen to it all. Do you think people would have had the guts to refuse, Mister? Well, no, we've been terrorized by her ever since the cursed day she learned to stand on her own two feet. You know we hated her, Mister, but no one dared stand up to her. She'd come walking up to you like a prison guard, stick her hands in her pants pockets, and say, looking you straight in the eye: "Wake up, Germaine! The new world is here, nothing will be the same again!" You'd sniffle to avoid dying of embarrassment, or you'd make as if to acquiesce with a vague nod of the head. And there she was, victorious—like some kind of a boxing champion—over at the neighbor's house. You held it against her, felt like throwing a basin of hot water in her face; that didn't make any difference, it would be exactly the same the next time, she'd be the duchess and you the worthless piece of shit. But that didn't keep her from turning up all of a sudden one day at your house with a nice box of chocolates. "Look what I've brought you, Germaine. Now, isn't good old Dominique sweet?"

And the evening Colonel Melun came, she was even more arrogant, more odious than ever.

"My suggestion," she said, "is that the main street of the village be named after him from now on."

"The streets of Romaincourt have never been named after anybody," retorted the mayor dryly. "And I don't see why it should start now."

"This is the golden opportunity to change that policy, Mister Mayor."

"The answer is no," especially since it is your suggestion... "Load up all this material and clear out of the square before I lose my temper!"

The mayor was the same age as she was; she couldn't intimidate him. Especially since he was the schoolteacher and had never heard of your uncle.

The week after that, she organized a demonstration with some oddballs from Paris who smoked hashish and played weird music. It was such a circus that the mayor called the gendarmerie. Being in police custody was nothing new to her, what with Indochina, Palestine, the right to birth control, abortion, the sheepherders of Larzac, gay marriage, and the improvement of tomato juice. You see, Mister, she tried to stuff our brains with all of the righteous causes from Paris. As if it were our fault that the Jews were gassed, Vietnam was bombed, the Indians exterminated, and the Africans enslaved. We weren't in Romaincourt anymore, Mister, but right in the middle of the Latin Quarter. And right up to the very end, she even had the gall to try to make us swallow her claim that the Tirailleur was her father. Having the main street of the village bear her father's name. Can you imagine where that would have led us, Mister?

Oh that Pinéguette brat, you're very lucky you never met her! Some people say she lost her senses due to the motorcycle accident that broke her femur when she was eighteen. But that's not true. She's been nuts ever since she left her mama's belly, that foul womb, which—according to Mâmiche Léontine—had been rid of a good number of runts before bringing *that thing* into the world. Right off the bat, people had a hard time deciding whether or not it was a girl. The mother, who never spoke to anyone, couldn't help them, and Dominique, the name she pinned on her, only added to the confusion and complicated things unnecessarily.

As long as she was alive, our nerves swung dangerously between fits of anger and bouts of exhaustion, from the dizzying heights of hysteria to the bottomless pits of depression. Then, with a typically Vosgian resignation, we grew accustomed to our sort. Our voices got calmer; our indignant looks became veiled with a mask of indulgence. We accepted the monster and listened to the widows coming back from the church muttering between their teeth, "Our Lord Jesus knows what he's doing. If he's sent this trial to us, it is to punish us for something."

We no longer paid any attention to her outbursts, her loud motorcycles and Rasta men, her insatiable appetite for whiskey and young dykes. Only the bell ringing out in the middle of the night still succeeded in irritating the most touchy villagers. But no matter how we tried to bar access to the church steeple, somehow she always managed to get up there.... From then on, people started treating her like a wild animal—granted, one that came from our parts, but wild nonetheless.

In short, a creature that is part of the family, one that is accursed yet loved: that peculiar feeling grew stronger after she went away to Paris. At first relieved that she was gone, we were soon filled with a feeling of emptiness. We were like gravely ill people who, upon leaving the hospital, regret having lost their hernia. It was so pronounced that the following Easter, the children started shouting when they recognized the sound of her motorcycle from a distance.

"Guess what? She's back!"

"So let her come back!" said the priest, irritated. "It couldn't be any worse than the blasted winter we just passed."

She came back, and then as soon as she headed back to Paris with the young Arab woman who'd accompanied her that time, the wall of silence fell back down between us. She and Etienne were the only ties that still held us together after sixty years of silence and hatred. Etienne, because he talked to everyone, and her, because everyone talked about her—in a bad way; there was nothing good to be said about her.

And yet if it hadn't been for her, nothing would have ever happened, Mister. Without her, we wouldn't be here shaking hands and unveiling plaques, receiving medals, walking back up the main street that now bears the name of an uncle you never knew.

Yes, it's all because of her, even though she never knew him either, by God! She was still suckling at her mother's breast when it all happened. Except that when she was almost seventeen, her head started wheeling round because of the photograph and everything Etienne had told her. Everyone but Etienne had forgotten the story he used tell out in the fields or in the evenings when there was a *couarail*-palaver. No one really listened to him, but he went on anyway without asking anyone's opinion. Yet Etienne knew perfectly well that no one wanted to hear any more about it, that it would just fuel resentment, open barely healed wounds, stir up unnecessary remorse, unavowed feelings of shame; those who weren't yet born at the time were beset with interminable fits of yawning as if he were relating the story of the Deluge or the fall of Babylon for the umpteenth time.

She disappeared two years after Colonel Melun's visit, but we knew it wasn't over with. Knew she'd be back, even more belligerent, more extravagant.

The next time, she didn't bring only placards and empty slogans. She came to provide us with a key element in the story of your uncle's life. He hadn't enrolled in Langeais, contrary to what we believed, but in Paris. Yes, he'd lived in the capital, and not just anywhere, but at the Paris mosque, rue Georges-Desplas. Without realizing it, she helped me resolve an enigma that had been running around in my head for sixty years.

You'll recall that he advised my parents not to send me to Nancy to pass my baccalaureate. Well, he succeeded in convincing my parents that I should become a seamstress, a suitable trade for a young girl of my age—can you believe it? He had a friend who taught sewing in a convent in Ménilmontant. My parents accepted on the condition that I come to see them at Christmas, Easter, and certain weekends, which posed absolutely no problem, since I was entitled to an official pass.

The day before I was to take the train, he approached me discreetly.

"Hey, Germaine, I have a few onions here—could you take them to my friends at the mosque in Paris?"

Onions, Mister, onions for the Paris mosque! Not carrots or turnips, not lamb or chicken, onions! At a time when the whole of France was tightening its *coriotte*-sash!

"But why onions?"

"Because... we like eating spicy food.... And also it's a custom of ours to give onions to the mosque. It favors divine blessings.... You need to go now, you'll miss your train...."

To think that I believed that taradiddle! He was fond of showing his affection for his friends and with good reason. But to make them a present of onions from the Vosges, or from Paris for that matter, when the Gestapo was snooping about everywhere!

However, it's very unlikely that he left directly from Paris to go to the front. The French army preferred to assign their Tirailleurs to the south, where they were less exposed to depression and tuberculosis. That hypothesis was confirmed by Colonel Melun's research. Your uncle was enlisted at the Paris Intendance and soon after was sent to Rochefort's colonial infantry depot for boot-training. From there he was assigned as private second class to the Twelfth Regiment of Senegalese Tirailleurs stationed for the winter at Sanary-sur-Mer in the department of Var.

In the beginning of the war, his regiment was stationed in the Ardennes region, first in Montmédy, and then in Beaumont-en-Argonne, where it encountered its first losses. Over a year to get from Langeais to Romaincourt. Dear Lord, what a circuitous route!

After having nursed and nourished him, the mayor put him up in the house standing over there in front of us. When your uncle came out of his delirium, the mayor helped him get settled and then handed him a bundle and told him in his gruff tone of voice, "Take off that uniform—you'll get us all bombed! You are no longer in the army; you're a farmhand. Here are your papers!"

Farmhand, my eye! In all his life here in Romaincourt, no one ever saw him out in a field, except on his bicycle, pedaling like mad and zigzagging through the trees without ever running into one. He'd disappear for several days and then pop back up again without warning, as if he'd materialized on the horizon, like the apparitions mentioned in the Bible. If he left heading north, he'd reappear in the south, and we never really knew whether he had passed by way of Afghanistan or the Berry region. The first few days he'd been nice and calm, because he was limping, because he didn't yet have a bicycle. In the morning, we'd see him go into the mayor's house to have his infusion. Then he'd walk around a bit and take a seat on the steps of the church muffled up in his greatcoat. Everyone went out to get a look at him, pretending they were going to the grocer's. The men chuckled under their breaths, and the children hid behind their mother's skirts.

Nonon Totor, who feared nothing, walked right up to him. "Here, have some macaroons. I wanted to offer you some chocolate-coated meringues that we call nigger-heads over here, but you've already got one."

The joke was heavy-handed but everyone giggled. Do you know what he did, Mister? He ate those macaroons, ate them slowly, ate them methodically, and when he'd finished, he took a few steps over to the fountain to rinse out his mouth and said, "Can anyone tell me how far we are from Chaumont?"

"Uh, it's a two-hour ride on horseback, Sir... at least I believe so," answered Cyprien Rapenne in an evidently intimidated tone of voice.

"Okay, you bunch of idiots, you can all go back home now."

Romaincourt split up. Everyone went back to their houses in silence, even Nonon Totor, who couldn't help grumbling, "Shit, you'd have thought we were a bunch of kids filing out of class under the watchful eye of the schoolmaster. That sure won't be the last he'll hear from me!"

He'd certainly earned his stripes. We never saw anyone make fun of him again, at least not to his face. That doesn't mean everyone liked him. He wouldn't have been denounced if that were the case. That doesn't mean there weren't racist remarks and shifty looks behind the scenes. We're in Romaincourt, Mister, a place with one hundred inhabitants who are all cousins, even if we haven't spoken to one another since the turn of the century. A closed community of failed marriages and property disputes. A small little corner of France brimming with jealousy, distrust, and suspicions, a place where everyone is hostile and grudges last a hundred years.

A tacit agreement had just been established between him and us: I'm black; I couldn't care less what you think. You be whatever you are—I won't get mixed up in your boozed-up gossip or your adultery problems. There's a war on. There's nothing we can do about that. This is what fate has determined: We're all in this together, even if you don't know it; we have to keep our noses to the grindstone—either die or survive together—whether you like it or not.

In the end, his life was no different from ours. There was his family, and then there was all the rest. His family was my own, the Tergoresses, and as I look at the street over there that now bears his name, I'm quite proud. When the Germans had him shot, we didn't lose a black man from the colonies who just happened to end up here when he escaped from the woods, but a brother, a cousin, an essential member of the clan, one of our blood and kin. My mother was his mother, and the same goes for my father. Uncle Louis, the mayor, was his uncle too, and my Nonon Totor, his nonon. He had an ordinary, sometimes even cordial relationship with the Rapennes, but I didn't hold that against him. I can't say as much for "that foreign girl." That's what we called her, Mister: "that foreign girl" or else "the sorceress" or simply Asmodée, as Totor had nicknamed her. She's the one who hatched that Pinéguette girl, Mister, because she married my other cousin, Pascal. Your uncle would spend his afternoons at her place, even after they found Pascal hanging from his belt in the barn. Oh, there was nothing fishy about it since they were neighbors and, as I told you, your uncle's house was attached to hers. He would sit down in the parlor and have her serve him an infusion and then he'd talk about the Germans. Asmodée sat shelling her broad beans, letting out innumerable and stupid "oh, you don't says!" Good old Pascal, who never said anything, but who was as gentle as a lamb, answered him with apologetic smiles and—as if in an attempt to ease the atrocities in this world—kindly opened the biscuit box and the honey jar for him. You might say I was jealous—all right, if you will; as far as Asmodée was concerned, I didn't mind being jealous. And anyway, she didn't deserve him; she never deserved anyone, and Pascal even less. Poor Pascal, she ruined his life. God only knows in what infamous street, what tawdry brothel he ran into that floozy! He told us he was going to join the journeymen of the Compagnons de France. He was a carpenter, Mister. Out of love for God and by the grace of Jesus, he transformed wood into pieces of gold, into wondrous objects. It wasn't craftsmanship but true art. Look at that commode over there: he made it just for me, and in the evening, when he'd finished chiseling, he would come and sit right there to recite Lamartine or play the accordion for me. And then one fine day, we received a card with these sparing words on it: *I've fallen deeply in love! Ask Germaine to forgive me.* He stayed away for another year, and when he came back, we saw he wasn't alone. And it wasn't just the two of them, Mister, but there was no denying they were three. A little blond child of five trotted along beside them, and it was evident from his looks and from his age that it couldn't have been Pascal's. The good Lord had fashioned that man into a shy and reserved being, but he was a smiling, obliging, and openhearted person who loved life—but that was before that miserable hussy got her hands on him. He parked his car, walked over to the porch to greet us, and then pointed to the other two who'd remained in the passenger compartment and said very abashedly, "Bernadette and Antoine, my family."

And that's when Nonon Totor announced with his typical brazenness that his father and brother, who were both railway workers, had been deported for having distributed communist tracts.... So then Pascal unloaded the luggage and went into his house and never came back out again.... It was a total eclipse, Mister, an eclipse. No more smiles, no more metal fittings or cornices, no more Lamartine, no more accordion!

He remained prostrate in his room, nibbling on honey biscuits and rarely going down to the parlor to be with his wife, who sat listening to love songs on the radio while filing her nails. When she grew tired of Jean Sablon, of Léo Marjane, and of Tino Rossi, she would go out to stroll around Martigny-les-

Bains or go shopping in the stores in Nancy. She never took the kid out except to go to Lamarche to see Dr. Couillaud. Up until the day she died, I always heard the villagers wondering whether Antoine coughed because his mama didn't take care of him, or if she didn't take care of him because he coughed.

They lived for a few months on the money Pascal had won with his Best Craftsman of France award, then food got scarce and she sold the Citroën.

It escaped no one's attention that she changed dresses much more often when the Tirailleur moved in so very nearby. But I can swear that nothing happened between them. Nothing. I would have found out about it one way or another. And yet she was interested in men; and he was interested in women.

He stopped in to see them several times a day, but it was to listen to "Tango de Marilou," by Robert Marino, or to talk Pascal into playing cards with him. She took the opportunity to show herself off to the best advantage and weave her treacherous web.

"You've lived in Paris—are you familiar with the Bal Nègre?"

"How could I not be familiar with the Bal Nègre, ma-dame?" He replied with that caustic irony he often used. "Except they immediately stuck me in this Tirailleur uniform, and since then I've become familiar with a whole different sort of dance hall."

As soon as Pascal grew weary of playing cards and went back up to his room, he would snatch one last biscuit and head for the door. She would stand in his way and begin cooing in her bewitching voice.

"Oh, so you only come for Pascal?"

He would nudge her away firmly with his elbow and go out without saying a word. No, nothing happened between them, nothing. What's more, Pinéguette was born exactly seven months to the day after his arrival and since nothing about her even vaguely suggested she was premature, West Indian, or Senegalese, she couldn't be his daughter, despite her bragging. I can assure you of that, Mister, she could not have been his daughter.

Obviously, we'll never know who the father was since the mother would take up with passersby as readily as she would with the Germans, and she debauched whole battalions of young men between Grand Ballon and the Vologne. Did anyone tell you that Antoine lost his innocence to her too?

And when their little business was finished, Antoine asked that tart, "So who's the father of your daughter?"

"Well, the black man, of course! Who else could it be?"

In the guise of proof, she'd taken out a photograph with Dominique at two weeks in your uncle's arms. On the back of the snapshot, scribbled with a Sergent-Major pen: *For Dominique, my daughter, with loving thoughts.*

And if people expressed any doubts, it was that piece of evidence Pinéguette would brandish, and if we remarked about the color of her skin, she would respond self-assuredly, "You'll see, I'll be as black as he was when I'm fifteen."

But she turned fifteen, and then thirty, and forty-five... and all the way up to the grave the poor girl remained as white and as pale as I am, without a single African trait appearing to corroborate her story.

Then the mayor offered him a bicycle, and he started playing the phantom in the Vosgian prairies while Pascal drank and beat his wife. She would scream and open the windows to spill her hatred out onto the roofs of Romaincourt, "You bunch of hicks, I'm going back to my country, back home! May God put a curse on you all! Every single one of you!"

However, since God is well-versed at his work, he put the curse on her instead. Little Antoine died of the croup, a veritable enemy of the Vosges, more deadly than winter and more feared than the Germans. It happened in the spring. At winter's end, Pascal went up to the barn and hung himself without leaving a note.

The wall of hatred surrounding Asmodée grew ever thicker. Since the money she got from the car had quickly melted away, and since she had no skills and no one within a hundred kilometers would lift a finger to help her, she would go out every night to rent herself to the Germans over there at the spa hotel in Martigny-les-Bains. A horse-drawn cart would come to pick her up and, curiously enough, she'd take the child along with her. She'd cross the street, her high heels clacking on the pavement with the even cadence of a clock. Then she'd pick up her progeny and duck quickly into the cart to escape from her pursuers, meaning a hundred or so pairs of eyes that were simultaneously glaring at her in hatred and contempt.

I was telling you that although he was very near to being a Tergoresse, some Rapennes would pay him a visit now and again and sometimes invite him over to their place. Cyprien in particular, who wasn't really such a bad sort, even though he was on the wrong side. He would walk right by this porch we're sitting on, go across the grass, and knock at your uncle's door. But he'd always greet me in passing.

"Hello, Germaine!"

"Hello, Cyprien!"

As a matter of fact, it isn't accurate to say that the Rapennes and the Tergoresses had broken all ties. We greeted one another, grudgingly I grant you, but we did. We'd see each other at baptisms, at marriages, communions. We are of the same blood after all. Originally, we were all Tergoresses. The Tergoresses founded this village, Mister, drawn by the advantages the castle presented, then one of them offered his daughter's hand to a man from Haute-Marne, and that's when the troubles began. His first grandchildren, Jean and Jean were the same age, were equally vigorous, and had the same stubborn temperament. One of them, the Tergoresse, was fairly good at school; the other, the Rapenne, was more like his father, more inclined to vegetable gardening and poaching. The Tergoresse, who passed his certificate at the end of primary school with flying colors, looked down upon his cousin and called him "*le petit Fougnat*," the no-account poacher.

In 1914 they'd both been mobilized. Jean Rapenne was transferred to the Somme and lived through the hell of the trenches, where he was seriously wounded. Jean Tergoresse on the other hand, being asthmatic, had been posted in Nancy and—with the help of the town's senator-mayor—become the secretary to the officer in charge of supplies. Traumatized by combat, disgusted with war, Jean Rapenne could no longer put up with his cousin, especially after Jean Tergoresse became president of the township's War Veterans Association and slightly embellished upon his heroic war deeds. The two men had had several altercations about the subject, and Jean Rapenne had been excluded from the meetings by the man he called "the Romaincourt draft-dodger." That's how our fratricidal war began.

You can't see it, no one from the outside can see it, but an invisible line separates us. See, from the edge of the pine forest all the way down to the war monument over there is Tergoresse territory, and from the war monument over to the railroad tracks is that of the Rapennes. You'll probably say all of this is white people's business, that it's Vosgian peasant folklore, that it has nothing to do with you. But you're wrong—you'll see that that ominous detail plays a part in your uncle's tragedy.

After Pascal's suicide, they refused to come to the funeral under the convenient pretext that taking one's life is not Christian, that Jesus would never forgive such an act. But two years earlier, when Cyprien's niece dropped a bastard, they had no qualms about organizing their baptism. And we all went to it, even if Jesus has never blessed that kind of progeny.

What must they have thought of him, they who'd never been pure of heart? Were they—as it was later rumored—the cause of his downfall? There's no way of telling because back in those days, everyone informed on everyone else. But you just can't picture that evil, cowardly, spiteful riffraff accepting the presence of a black man in their region; not just any black man, but a soldier who was protected by the Tergoresses, a soldier who never stayed put, who was up to fishy business that was likely to infuriate the occupiers. Sweet Jesus, I have no proof to accuse them with, but none either to proclaim their innocence! You alone can decide, when the time comes, back over there standing before the justice of heaven.

It was them, I'm sure of it, the anonymous letters to the Kommandantur in Epinal claiming that Totor was defrauding on taxes he owed to the occupier, that Mâmiche Léontine was putting up Alsatians (we call them "Haguenaux" here), and that the Colonel had a firearm buried in his garden. How could anyone know all those details if they weren't from Romaincourt? Impossible to even think for a second that a Tergoresse would turn another Tergoresse over to the enemy. Only the Rapennes would be capable of such an ignoble deed, Mister.

Your heart would have to be nearly full up with rancor to go so far as to inform on the Colonel! The Colonel was the only stranger in the village, except for your uncle, of course. He came from Vroncourt-la-Côte, the birthplace of Louise Michel—a distant cousin of his—but he'd married a girl from here, a descendant of the chatelain. After she died, he preferred to stay in order to flower her grave. Your uncle shared both the Colonel's military vocation and his passion for playing checkers. Moreover, the Colonel knew the colonies as well as he did the narrow streets of Romaincourt. He was a jovial, yet melancholy man who never left his château except to care for his horse or gallop around the countryside singing military songs. One fine morning, Romaincourt was quite surprised to see him come out of his home, walk along beside the church and the grocery store past the water tank and the war memorial, and go up to the mayor's door.

"What's this I hear about a soldier being within our walls and no one thinking to advise the hierarchy?"

"Oh, Colonel," apologized the mayor, also stifling his laughter, "it's entirely my fault—your neighbors have nothing to do with it."

"In that case, the mayor of Romaincourt is assigned to spud peeling and will execute a one-hundred-kilometer march!"

"Yes, sir!"

They burst out in roaring laughter, then the Colonel went on, "All right, take me to the black man. I can't wait to meet him."

The mayor took him directly upstairs to the room where he'd been laid in a wooden bed with a horsehair mattress. They found him reclining, eyes open, gazing up at the ceiling. He was undoubtedly daydreaming since he didn't hear them come in and the mayor had to touch his shoulder before he startled, proving at last that he was alive.

"I've brought someone to see you."

He propped himself up on his elbow to look at the newcomer.

"Don't move so much, you'll hurt yourself. Colonel Michel, Bernard Michel!"

"Pleased to meet you, Colonel," answered your uncle, grimacing in pain as he held out his hand.

The Colonel put his glasses on and bent over his bandaged wounds with a concerned expression.

"He was in sad shape when he arrived—"

"But, Mister Mayor," cut in the Colonel, "Mercurochrome is simply not enough in a case like this. Wait here. I've got what it takes!"

He rushed over to the little wooden staircase that swayed dangerously under his heavy hobnailed shoes, clomped through the cold empty room at the bottom that was meant to be a parlor if there had been any furniture to put in it. The Colonel marched resolutely up the slope, his tall silhouette stooping to avoid the snow-laden branches of the trees, and disappeared through the carriage gate that led to the château. Ten minutes later, he retraced his steps carrying a tube that he handed to the mayor.

"Here, this is penicillin. Our man will heal quickly with this. And you must give him twice that many blankets: of all living creatures, these people are the most sensitive to Koch's bacillus. Are you questioning what I say?"

"Oh, I'd never dream of it, Colonel!"

"Fine, I'll leave him with you. I need to get back to my horse."

He turned toward the patient. "Are you fond of tea? Do you enjoy playing checkers? If so, you'll pay me a visit." Pointing at the bandages, he added, "But not right away, of course."

When his wounds healed and he had the strength to go down the stairs and set foot outside, we were the first ones he came to visit, before the Colonel and even before the mayor. No one—neither him nor us—had done anything to make that happen. It was simply that we were his closest neighbors, since his door opened onto our street, whereas in order to communicate with Pascal's family, he had to walk down the sidewalk of the main street. I caught sight of him as I was busily staring out the window observing the play of colors the sunlight was making in the icicles hanging from the branches. He walked across the street and strode right up to our house, gave three sharp raps on the door. I went running into the parlor, where my parents were listening to the radio.

"What is it?" asked my mother in a panic.

"He's here!"

"Who's here, dear God?"

"It's him, Papa, the black man!"

He was still standing at the door, his arms crossed over his chest, kicking his shoes up against the porch steps to make the snow fall off. Papa opened the door and had him come in. He took off his greatcoat and sat slowly down in the chair we offered him.

"It's nice and warm in here. That's why I've come, and to chat a little too."

"I see. The Colonel told us you were more resistant to tuberculosis than to solitude."

"And those of us who have no one left to talk with begin talking to the trees."

"We are a people of silence."

"Silence stems from winter."

"Not from blood?"

He started laughing as he took the cup of chicory that Mama was holding out to him. I already noticed the very first day that every time he was asked a question that made him uncomfortable, he'd let out a vague, instinctive chuckle.

"How are things at your place?"

"The roof keeps the snow out and the woodstove is holding up, Mr. Tergoresse."

"I'm sure you'll soon get used to things here."

"One doesn't get used to the winter, Madame. As for all the rest, I won't be fussy. Poke out one of your eyes if you want to live with the Cyclops, my mother used to say. Is Chaumont far from here?"

"Oh, I've never really looked into it. We'll have to ask—isn't that so, Adelaide? Er, yes, her name is Adelaide, and I'm Leon, Leon Tergoresse, and this is our daughter, Germaine."

"I don't need to introduce myself—everyone already knows who I am," and he flashed his white teeth in a great burst of laughter.

Papa merely smiled as he leaned over the radio to turn up the sound. Lys Gauty was singing "Le chaland qui passe," then the commentator announced some news briefs. We heard that Robert Baden-Powell, the founder of the Scout Movement, had died and that all Frenchmen born in 1921 were to spend eight months in Youth Work Camps. Then a children's choir sang "Maréchal, nous voilà" in hoarse, breathless voices. A long speech followed: Petain was inaugurating a kindergarten.

"Do you believe this Franco-German friendship will last?"

"The hyena and the billy goat are fated to get along, Mr. Tergoresse, at least as long as one has its hoof in the other's mouth."

"Does everyone speak in that manner in Africa?"

"Only the older people, Madame."

"What will you do after the war?"

"Go back to Guinea, found a hostel for Africans in Paris, think about getting married... I don't know. For the time being, the war is still on."

"But the war is over, sir!"

"Well, then, it needs to be sparked up again!"

"Oh, you talk like those people in London."

"The people in what?"

"Oh, some fanatics that have gone over to England to allegedly liberate us from the Germans. Well, Mister, I say that if they want to liberate us from the Germans, they should go anywhere but England. Has anyone ever seen an Englishman liberate anyone from anything? I'm sorry, I'm letting myself get worked up."

"Have you ever been to London?"

"Uh, no!" He pointed to the wireless set. "Only through the radio! You can come listen to it if you like. I can receive them from eight p.m. on. It'll cure you of your loneliness."

"I'll come, since I don't have much to do during the day, and even less so at night. Thank you, Mr. Tergoresse. Nothing like a good conversation to cheer a man up. See you soon!"

"Come over whenever you feel like having a bite, if there's one to be had. The cold has frozen the vegetables, the mildew has rotted the potatoes, and when we have a few pounds of wheat, the Germans come and fill their bellies with it. France is perishing, Mister—the Jerries have condemned it to death, not by war, but by hunger."

In the meantime, he'd picked up his greatcoat and was making to open the door when he put his hand to my cheek and asked, "Are you in high school, Germaine?"

I was going to open my mouth, but my mother had already answered in my place.

"She was supposed to pass her baccalaureate in Nancy, but..."She didn't finish the sentence and simply lifted her arms skyward.

"You know you can give me your clothes to wash."

"The fact is I don't have any clothes, Madame."

He laughed again, with that same unleashed, energetic, and infectious laughter as shortly before in the parlor, then he took a few steps and disappeared down at the bottom of the main street after turning the corner at the washhouse.

"I'm sure he's going to the mayor's house," murmured my mother.

"Where else do you expect him to go?"

That was the night Cyprien Rapenne's chicken house burned down.

The Colonel had him over a few days later. Since he was taking his sweet time showing up, the Colonel came to get him himself. As they were going past our place, Papa cracked a joke.

"That's not fair, Colonel! You're making off with our guest just when we've gotten hold of a few ounces of meat."

"Don't worry, I'll get him back to you as soon as possible. It's become more difficult for us to feed ourselves than to defeat the Germans. Everyone is on a strict diet, even the hierarchy!"

What we called the "château" was in truth a large imposing house thattowered over the rest of the village. You first entered the edifice through a vast room containing a collection of bizarre objects, tools that the Colonel undoubtedly used to fashion medals with. They were of all forms and colors. Some seemed to resemble presses, others punches; still others pincers, awls, braces, but they all emanated a smell of wax and molten metal. Then a spiral staircase led up to the mezzanine where the reception room was and where the Colonel entertained his rare visitors, offering them tea and a game of checkers. And one could just imagine the numerous rooms above in which no one had ever set foot and which had always fueled incredible legends. Stories of vampires back in the days of our grandfathers, stories of mummies since the Colonel had been there, especially since his wife had died. Perhaps it wasn't really his wife in that grave but only a few kilograms of medals. He had probably embalmed her and put her in the middle of one of those large rooms decorated with red carpets, Hindu statues, and candelabras where he would spend the night reciting poems to her.

A thin young woman, unkempt but beautiful, was his *bâbette*-servant, and quite a lot of gossip went around about the two of them.

When they reached the reception room, the Colonel rang a bell and the *bâbette* appeared in all of her pallor at the foot of the sumptuous oak stairway laid with a long strip of red carpet edged with golden yellow fringe.

"Did you call for me, sir?"

"Serve us some tea, Odette, and try to find us something to eat, something good—I'm receiving a hero."

Then he walked over to the billiard table and unfolded a military map.

"I heard about the exploits of the Twelfth RTS. Would you please elucidate?"

He placed lead soldiers on either side of a line reaching from the Ardennes to the Vosges and handed the baton to your uncle.

"It's quite simple, Colonel, this is where we were on the night of the thirteenth to the fourteenth. Brutal skirmishes at the break of dawn. Our first heavy losses, sir. That night we began our retreat between the Saulx and the Ornain.

"But, good God, given the positions and the swiftness of the enemy, why didn't you retreat in the afternoon?"

"A path of retreat had to be found first. There were refugees coming from all sides, Colonel, and those idiots didn't know which way to go!"

"Between the Saulx and the Ornain just like between a rock and a hard place!"

"Staff sergeants don't give the orders, sir."

It was no longer a billiard table but a veritable battlefield that they had become completely engrossed in, mind and soul. Odette, who was undoubtedly afraid of being wounded with the sharp points of their jargon, was circling around them as one would around a barbed-wire barrier. She dusted off an end table, adjusted a curtain, and served drinks and appetizers they were oblivious to.

"During the night, our forward units reached the Andelot-Neufchâteau transverse while the rear units were on the Joinville-Houdelaincourt line."

"Uh-huh, not bad, not bad! Let's see... I fully understand your position on the bridge at Harréville, but my God, the HQ at Vrécourt? Wouldn't it have been better to have it in Malaincourt?"

"Throughout the day of the seventeenth, everything was calm. At nineteen hundred, orders came to continue the retreat toward Bains-les-Bains. At midnight, there were counter-orders: we were to retrace our steps and reoccupy the positions we'd just abandoned. On the eighteenth, our HQ was transferred to Malaincourt."

"Finally!"

"Close to midnight, another counter-order..."

"Ah, the fault of our military schools, Sergeant Major! Examination standards have gone downhill. Did you see their military communiqués? Chock-full of spelling errors. No, no, it was written in the stars: we could never have won this war."

Just then he started and stared wide-eyed around the room in bewilderment as if he'd just landed there.

"Oh, thank you, Odette! Listen to that, Sergeant Major!"

And Addi Bâ heard a melodious and rousing tune that he'd never had the occasion to listen to before.

"A Lebanese march, military music from that distant land! Completely different from what one hears over here!"

He invited him to sit down and served him milk with grenadine syrup since he didn't drink alcohol.

Odette began with a dandelion salad, then she brought in a delicious leg of lamb, served with green vegetables and, to top things off, a platter of strong Cancoillotte cheese decorated with diced pears.

"Don't mention this on the outside, you could get me lynched. It's simply in honor of the warrior of the Meuse that I've brought out my pre-war buffet. Tomorrow, believe me, it'll be stale bread and leek soup...

"From what colony, Sergeant Major?"

The question was so abrupt that your uncle didn't understand immediately.

"Sudan, Dahomey, Congo?"

"Guinea! French Guinea, Colonel!"

"Ah, the source of the Niger and the Senegal rivers, the isthmus of Kaloum, the Fouta Djallon mountain range! What village?"

"Bomboli! Pelli-Foulayabé to be precise, a nearby hamlet."

"Bomboli, that's near Pita! Not to be confused with Bombori, which is in Oubangui-Chari, on the border of Sudan, and especially not with Bombona, which is in Haute-Volta, not far from the Gold Coast!"

"Chapeau, Colonel! You know the land better than I do."

Before walking him to the door, the Colonel showed him the portrait of a woman hanging over the piano.

"A distant cousin, deported for a time to New Caledonia for subversive activities. If they'd asked me to execute her, I would have done so without hesitating. Wouldn't you, Adjutant?"

"Yes, of course, Colonel, of course I would."

"Aha! I knew that would be your answer. Your uniform is superfluous: one can see from a distance you're a born soldier!"

— § —

Papa, with the help of the mayor, went to great lengths to obtain ration cards for him and find shoes that fit him. Mama brought the old pillowcases, curtains, sheets, and grandfather's jackets up from the cellar. I took the time to make him shirts and pants as well as two cloth jackets and a coat of rabbit fur. In addition to that, I knitted him pullovers and ankle socks. But I'd gone to all that trouble for naught. He kept on wearing his Tirailleur uniform in spite of the mayor's disapproval, in spite of the fear it inspired in his neighbors. Imagine what might have happened to us due to him if we hadn't been here in Romaincourt, this little town in the middle of nowhere, where nothing ever happened, no one ever came, not even the bombs, not even the Germans' dogs, not even the rumblings that were shaking the world?

Yet he did venture out beyond the town limits as soon as Papa had the misfortune of giving him a bicycle (it was in fact the one my cousin Andre, Pascal's brother, had bought just before he and his father were deported), and from then on Romaincourt was in grave danger. Riding around perched atop his bicycle over hill and over dale through the occupied Vosges mountains wearing that uniform, can you believe it?

"Take that off, take it off for God's sake! You'll get us all executed!" the mayor would scream at him.

He'd wear civilian clothes for a few days, but he would quickly fall back into his old ingrained soldier habits, and, once again, the Colonel would rejoice while the mayor tore his hair out. How, in spite of all that, did Romaincourt escape the Gestapo's reprisals? That question, which was often on people's minds, would make Mâmiche Léontine boiling mad.

" *Oye, oye, oye*! Aie-aie-aie! That *Jestapo* has just got to leave him in peace. He has the right to put on whatever *affûtiaux*-getup he wants to!"

"It's not just any *affûtiaux*-getup, Mâmiche! It's a uniform, war fatigues!"

At times like that, she'd never answer me. She only answered when she knew she'd end up being right. The way she saw it, Gestapo or no Gestapo, your uncle just couldn't be wrong, no matter what. She simply called him "the Sergeant" because in her Alsatian mouth, it was much simpler to pronounce.

The first time he came to her house, she'd merely motioned to a seat and held out a cup of *aouatte,* the watered-down chicory that was our lot. Then she'd gone back to her embroidery and, after a good long while, had uttered words that were incomprehensible to him, *"Z'avez vu la chaouée de ce matin?* Didya heed the drencher this morning?" Just to break the heavy silence that had begun to oppress them.

"Your embroidery is so delicate, Mâmiche."

"So you call me Mâmiche too? Well, then, there'll be two of you along with Germaine, since the Jerries went and took Andre off and Pascal doesn't say much anymore."

"Would you like me to help you?"

"You know how to embroider?"

"My father taught me. You know, Mâmiche, where I'm from, embroidery is a man's job. The noblest of all trades, my father used to say."

" *Môn!* Lord! You mean your women have all deserted you?"

"Embroidering has nothing to do with them, Mâmiche!"

"I wouldn't like to set eyes on that, a man doing embroidery!"

At first, she was probably standoffish, intimidated, and he was so reserved, he always made people who didn't know him very well feel as if he looked down on them, as if he were *nâreux,* as we say around here—stuck-up. It took them quite some time, a very long time, to break the ice. After that, he'd come over to her house every evening to embroider, gulp down his *frichti*-grub or simply chat about the snow, the rain, and then the rain some more.

She lived in that half-timbered house you see at the top of the main street, the last house on this side of the village, just before you reach Sapinière ridge. Papa, who venerated the bonds of blood, would nod toward it every morning, his voice filled with welling pride.

"There it is, the cradle of the Tergoresses!"

His mother had devotedly accepted and passed on the blood that flows in our veins, hoeing and weeding, grinding and scrubbing from morning to night, obstinate and silent like all women in her time, submissive to the clan, loyal to her husband. She was a true Lorraine, in spite of her distant Alsatian origins. In just one year, she'd succeeded in becoming an integral part of Romaincourt, adopting the *patenasse*—a quilted winter bonnet—without a fuss, the macaroons and the bergamot, the ancient rasping patois that she pronounced with Alsatian tones, arousing the scorn of the folks down the hill (meaning the Rapennes), who still called her "the foreigner" even after she'd been here for almost half a century. She'd accepted the harsh, wind-whipped insular life, harrowed by wars and snowstorms, molded by routine and promiscuity. She'd carried out her duties as wife and mother to the very end, even more efficiently after the death of Pâpiche than during his lifetime. And here she was holding out a symbolic baby bottle, doing her best to provide both roots and shelter to this African whom no one had expected and who had neither brother, nor sister, nor mother, nor property in his homeland—a distant continent from here. This black man who had nothing but the dreary hush of the snow, nothing but the bottomless pit of the war.

I remember her asking him one day—not daring to look him in the eye, "Had you ever seen snow before you came here?"

"Oh, yes. In Langeais!"

"Had the war already started over there?"

"No, I was just a boy."

"Do you mean you grew up over there?"

"I'm sorry, Mâmiche. I arrived there when I was thirteen years old."

"You left Africa all alone when you were thirteen?"

"No, I came with my father—I mean the man I was supposed to call my father."

"Was he a Tirailleur too?"

"You don't understand, Mâmiche, that father was white, just like you, like Germaine, like the snow outside the window."

Mâmiche gulped noisily and fell silent. That's the way Mâmiche was: she would clam up in silence when things got dangerous and complicated. They continued embroidering while I busied myself boiling the chestnuts. The conversation struck back up again a good quarter of an hour later, but slipped prudently over to less puzzling, less mind-wearying subjects. We shared the piece of black bread and the hot puréed chestnuts, and when it was time to go, Mâmiche mounted a fresh attack.

"You mean to tell me that despite your appearance, your father was a white man?"

"That's perfectly correct."

"How can that be?"

"Because of the witch doctor."

"The witch doctor?"

"The witch doctor, Mâmiche!"

The next day he came back to do some embroidery and wolf down his *frichti*. When Mâmiche saw he was readying to leave, she knotted her apron as if she were preparing for a fight.

"Now that we've gotten to know each other, could you come out and tell me, what we're supposed to call you?"

"Addi! Addi Bâ!"

And before long the children no longer whimpered and hid their eyes, nor did the men hasten their pace and the old women stopped lurking behind their curtains when they saw him pass. In just a few months, by some mysterious magical feat, he had become a familiar part of the landscape, like the façade of the church or the pillars of the washhouse. Even the *cheûlard*-boozers from Chez Marie, who spent their time draining their cups of moonshine and making lame jokes about anything unfamiliar to them, changed subjects and attitudes.

He became one of the villagers of Romaincourt, just like Nonon Totor and I; he had breakfast at the mayor's, lunch with us, and dinner at Mâmiche's; he received visits from Yolande Valdenaire and went to play a game of checkers at the Colonel's two or three times a week,.

The only thing that still differentiated him from the rest of us was that damned Tirailleur uniform, the horrid getup that had the peculiar effect of breaking the mayor's heart. Your uncle would spend his afternoons at Pascal's house and, after the baby—I mean Pinéguette—was born, it became a veritable ritual. We didn't actually call her that yet; we'd say "Pascal's little girl" or simply Dominique—the name that slut of a mother had given her. He'd go listen to Robert Marino sing "Tango de Marilou" ten times over while he talked to Pascal or cuddled the abandoned child, whose mother would often go shopping—if you see what I mean. I must admit he'd become the only thing that tied that house over there to the rest of the village. Nobody wanted to have anything to do with that slut, and as far as Pascal was concerned, well—we respected his wish to cut himself off from the world, especially since it broke our hearts to see the state that she-devil had left him in.

It's understandable that, growing up, she came to believe he was her true father, especially because of that photograph, especially because after Etienne's first marriage, he blabbed around in the *couarails*-palavers—repeating even to those who didn't want to hear it—what that whore had told him while the two of them were under the pine trees, stretched out on the needles, as close as two hairs and as naked as if they'd just been born. But she'd just said that to show off, to impress that sucker Etienne, who'd been parachuted into life with no guide and with no knowledge of women.

People knew it was impossible, knew she just couldn't be his daughter. Your uncle arrived here in early January, she was born the following fourth of July. Explain how she could have been his offspring when nothing can prove it, nothing: nothing to suggest she was a premature child, nothing that resembled the sun-browned faces of Africa! Later, when she was about to turn eight and people pointed that out to her, she jumped up on her two feet like an endangered kitten, eyes ablaze, and spat in our faces, "You'll see how black I'll be when I'm ten!"

And when she was ten, we heard, coming out of that same little mouth, "You'll see how black I'll be when I'm fifteen!"

It's understandable that she ended up believing it: he was the only person who'd ever touched her little body with anything that resembled a caress. Especially since the conviction her mother once nurtured—that she might have been Pascal's child—quickly proved to be erroneous in the face of the obvious. Standing before a mirror, the child reflected nothing resembling Pascal. If at least she'd taken after her mother! If she ever did look like anyone, uh, well, it was someone that had never been seen in this township.

Her life was sheer hell from the cradle to the grave, Mister. But was it our fault if everyone was hostile toward her, if she left school under a hail of projectiles and jeers from her young schoolmates?

"Get that bitch baby up on the roof! The bitch baby up on the roof!" they would call after her.

No, it had nothing to do with us. She was baseborn, born under a curse, and that curse pursued her till the very end!

Poor Romaincourt, we didn't know what we were doing—we were far from thinking it would backfire! No one was discerning enough to notice that by the time she was about ten, she'd become a veritable little wildcat: with red eyes, a ferocious heart, the biceps of a lumberjack, and five-inch-long claws. By that time, she was able to vomit the torrents of bile we'd relentlessly dumped on her from her birth back up in our faces. She began by setting the hogs on fire, opening up the stables, and untying the cattle. Then she smeared our windows with excrement and went up into the church steeple to ring the bells. At seventeen she set the silo on fire, and at twenty rewarded us with her first sit-in.

"He was sold out to the Germans, and when they executed him, we didn't do anything for him: didn't give him a medal or an honorable mention, didn't even dedicate a bit of a plaque to his memory. Do you know why? Because he was black. Damned racists!"

We didn't understand what she meant. To us, she'd simply found another good opportunity to make us look like idiots.

Now that she's dead, now that you've come, and a lovely plaque is shining on the house where he used to live—the same house she grew up in—it's not really the same anymore. No one around here knew what they were doing, no one had any idea we were sheltering a hero. Heroes aren't heroes until they're dead, are they?

Except, that Pinéguette never explained anything; she just bullied.

And at the time, he was far from the grave. He'd get up early, go over to the mayor's, then to Mâmiche's, then he'd come here to listen to the radio, and from time to time, we'd see him disappear under the carriage gate of the château for a game of checkers. And then, without our really knowing why, he became that phantom perched up on that bicycle whom we'd see coming and going without daring to ask any questions.

Mâmiche, who used to worry about everything, would murmur in my ear as if she were revealing a code, "Go see what the Sergeant is up to over at his place. He hasn't come for his *frichti* for three days."

"Mâmiche, that Sergeant of yours disappeared three days ago, and we haven't seen him reappear yet. And don't ask me where he's gone, God only knows."

Yolande Valdenaire stopped by from time to time to bring him potatoes or radishes. By that time he was calling her "Mama" and she called him "Son." She'd tiptoe in, go furtively up to join him in his room. Then he would walk her to the door, where they would remain for a minute or two whispering to one another; we had no idea what about.

"Those two are getting closer and closer," fretted Mâmiche Léontine behind her curtains. "We'll end up finding out what they're digging at."

And we did in fact end up finding out, but only after their death because Etienne spilled the beans and the city folks started writing things down.

The first time he came to our house, he'd hardly paid any attention to the crackling of the radio, but months later things had changed. He would come over at eight p.m., hurry into the living room, turn his head in the direction of the kitchen to greet Mama and me. Then he'd sit down beside Papa and turn the radio button without even asking permission.

Well, that was certainly no time to disturb him! He was glued to the set, eyes dilated, ears pricked up. And you could tell, he just wasn't there anymore, his mind had taken flight, gone off to mingle with the complicated network of wires filling the radio. You could have put a hot coal to his cheek, he wouldn't have felt it. Then the voice on the radio fell silent, his face took on a worried look, and you could see anxiety running over his eyelids and through his fingers. He would throw up his arms in despair, bolt down whatever supper there was, and go off to bed looking like a hunter coming back empty-handed from the blind.

Those dull, enigmatic evenings followed one after the other for a good long while. We would listen to speeches, then to music, then speeches, then music, but on one particular evening, there were no more speeches or news briefs. A simple sentence pronounced as if by the lofty voice of a Greek god cut in to the music: "Trust in the thorn!"

He only listened to it once. This time he stood up calmly, said good-bye to Mama and Papa, touched me on the cheek, and went out into the pitch-black night. It was his first prolonged absence. It lasted one or two weeks. Back then, it wasn't easy to count the days. Everything was head over heels, even the good Lord's logbook.

The world was like a pot of ratatouille that some long celestial spoon had spent weeks stirring. Chunks of Africa and Asia here in the Vosges, splinters of the Vosges fallen over there in Zululand! All you had to do was venture out as far as Vittel or Epinal, to realize that. We'd see Croatian and Slovenian conscripts marching by alongside German troops. There were the Africans, the Malagasies, and the Indochinese, all deployed to collect war booty. There were even Hindus taken prisoner in Dunkirk while they were fighting in the English army, who later rode by in SS sidecars chanting: "England quit India! Long live independent India!"

That particular period is less familiar to me, as I soon left for Paris. I only came back to Romaincourt five or six times, I only know what I was told after the war.

I learned from the newspapers that the English had dropped Gaullist tracts and balloons containing the free press all over the region. I also knew from Mama's letters that Addi Bâ was growing tenser, more mysterious, more absent by the day. I have absolutely no knowledge about that period in his life. There are a lot of things I don't understand. For example, why did he remain in his house when he knew the Jerries were after him? The life of that kind of man is not easy to sum up, Mister: it's too vast, too convoluted, too incomprehensible, like a great river! He knew so many people, went so many places before he came face-to-face with History! When it comes right down to it, he led a double, even a triple life, counting Romaincourt. There was the life everyone knew about that he lived between the château and the town hall, between the main street and rue Jondain, between Church Street and School Street. But then there was all the rest that was deeply obscure: his life as a Don Juan and the one he led as a member of the Resistance. There was the part of his life we suspected of being terribly wicked, the part that incited us to cast winks at each other and murmur under our breaths, and then there was the mysterious part, that we had inklings about, but never spoke of.

Anyway, whispers were rapidly diverted away from that hussy, since it turned out that he'd remained loyal to Pascal to the very end and that he wasn't the father of the little girl. People brought up other women, a widow in Roncourt, a young girl in Vittel, an elegant lady in Martigny-les-Bains, another widow in Fouchécourt... He was, after all, young, vigorous, elegant, exotic, and the war had left no dearth of lonely women, what with soldiers dying on the front lines and recalcitrant recruits being deported by the occupying forces. No one could hold anything against him. He enjoyed women and they reciprocated. Even Totor carefully avoided the awkward subject. I only heard him make a remark once; he'd just come back from Chez Marie and had had quite a lot to drink.

"I'm not surprised the Sergeant's not here. You know, that guy's *broyotte*-fly is wide open!"

But the next spring, something unusual happened in Le Café de l'Univers, a dimly lit bar in Martigny-les-Bains. That evening two men were sipping glasses of plum brandy, talking in low voices, when a fairly elderly gentleman awkwardly made his way in, hesitated quite some time before closing the door, and walking over to a table. He took off his coat and gloves, set his large wire-rim glasses straight, rubbed his hands energetically together, letting out a cloud of misty breath, set his heavy black bag under the table, and slowly unfolded his newspaper without looking either toward the counter where Alfred—the proprietor—was busying himself, or in the direction of the clients, most of whom were playing cards and drearily puffing on their corn paper Gitanes.

"A cup of coffee, please!" said the stranger when Alfred shuffled over to his table.

The surprised look of the owner and the laughter that broke out at the other tables refreshed his memory.

"Oh, sorry, a cup of tea… or chicory, or…"

"Burnt brandy!" decided the owner. "Burnt brandy with honey! That's the only hot drink I've got!"

"Fine, burnt brandy it is!"

"Pretty cold spring!" someone remarked.

"Let 'em have the potatoes and the wheat if they want, but they gotta leave us the moonshine!" chuckled someone else.

Alfred went back to his post, turned the knob on the radio, and stuck his ear up to the front of it without paying any more attention to the stranger.

"Can't make out a word!"

He tapped on the set to stop the unpleasant crackling sounds it was emitting, then lifted his head and switched it off, looking annoyed.

"We can't even pick up Vichy anymore!"

The sound of glasses clinking, of hands slapping cards down on the table, and the clatter of dishes that Alfred was washing as he whistled a haunting song could be heard much more clearly.

Someone brought up Doriot's recent visit to Epinal.

"What's the world coming to?" cried Alfred furiously. "Can you believe it? They've stolen two thousand five hundred ration tickets in Xertigny! Two thousand five hundred!"

"Ah, the loafers! What can they do with them in London? It's just to take the bread out of our mouths!"

Then Alfred, who was beginning to put the chairs on the tables, winked at the two men and shouted so everyone would hear, "By God, the man with the glasses forgot his bag!"

"It's all right, Alfred," answered one of the two men. The man's a neighbor of ours; we'll take the bag back to him."

"Good, that makes things simple! Come on, boys, I'm closing up now.Do your best not to get waylaid by those saboteurs from London."

He passed in front of the two men, pretending to be sweeping the floor, and mumbled as clearly as he could, "To get back to Lamarche, take the road via La Virolle!"

The two men jumped on their bicycles and disappeared into the night. At the edge of the forest, a red light followed by a green one flashed through the darkness. They put on the brakes so abruptly, they almost went tumbling head over heels.

A figure stepped out of the forest and walked toward them. It was a man shining his flashlight in his own face: the same fellow with the hat and glasses of a little earlier in the café.

"I was supposed to make sure that it was you who got the bag.... You'll be Simon, and you, Alex! Here take these, one never knows!"

He held out two pistols wrapped in newspaper.

"Someone will come and leave you a message: follow his instructions closely!"

"The bag?" ventured the one who was now to be called Simon.

"Leaflets, lots of leaflets and instructions on how to organize meetings, procedures to follow, establishing passwords, mailboxes! All right, off with you! Are you sure you can trust the guy in the bar?"

"He's with us, don't worry!"

"Fine, Simon, fine!"

He went back into the woods and before disappearing murmured: "One more thing, don't try and contact me. I'll take care of that. Otherwise, Simon, Alex, you can call me Gauthier. Gauthier, got it?"

The two others grunted in assent and got back on their bicycles.

The next morning, Simon—alias Marcel Arbuger—found an envelope in his mailbox. *La parole à l'Evangile* (The Word of the Gospel). A password undoubtedly. The message didn't stop there. There was also a map of the towns, bridges, roads, isolated farms, and intersections, all traced in violet and red ink. Under the map scale, a date and time. The following Tuesday, Alex and he stood in front of a rustic wooden gate with "The Boène Farm" burned into it with a hot iron. Simon rapped five times on the gate, spacing the last two raps far apart. There was the sound of coughing and then of a dog barking. A stout, slightly stooped middle-aged man came toward them following the beam of his flashlight.

"Whose word?"

"That of the Gospel."

"All right, come in."

It was a farm the likes of which you see everywhere in the Vosges, with a house in the center and everything else arranged around it: the stables, the barn, the silo, and the tool shed.

The man directed them toward an outbuilding located in back near the pasture fence.

"Hey, Helene, serve us something to drink in the barn, and tell the boy to come with the present."

They emptied half a bottle of moonshine and nibbled on a slab of bacon.

"So what is this present?"

The boy tore open the brown paper wrapped around a cylinder-shaped object the size of a small suitcase.

"Gosh!" Simon whistled. "A roneo! They sure aren't pulling any punches! We can compete with Goebbels's propaganda with this!"

"They thought it best to hide it here. It's less risky. No one but the roe and the fallow deer ever comes around here. See how big the barn is? We can put up a hundred or a hundred and fifty men without raising suspicions."

"Let's go up and see."

"No, you are to take care of the roneo and the boys. Alex will manage the leaflets. The rest is up to Him."

"Who, Him?"

"That's not for me to say."

They hooked up the machine, stuck a ream of paper in it before putting the carbon paper and the ink in. The results were conclusive. The mechanism was a true wonder, be it in a country barn or in the depths of a forest.

Just as they were about to leave, Simon ventured to ask the question that had been burning his lips.

"When will we be able to see Him?"

The farmer hesitated, cast a wary look about the barn.

"Tuesday, at eighteen hundred, a woman will be waiting for you near the fountain in Saint-André-les-Vosges. She'll have a black scarf on her head, a gray coat, and a parasol in her left hand.

"Tell her, 'Our uncle baptized the baby boy.'"

"She'll answer, 'I know. How strange for a secularist!'"

One week later, following instructions the woman with the black scarf had given, they walked up the steps to the church in Romaincourt, where they found your uncle sitting muffled up in his legendary greatcoat.

"For the golden chanterelles?"

"Go see Totor!"

He stood up, slipped a folded paper into Simon's hand, and disappeared.

"But it's a black man!" exclaimed Alex.

Simon simply answered, "This is war."

It all seems ridiculous today, but it didn't back then. I'll have you know, Mister, that children were arrested for having taken a swastika off a wall, men and women were deported for listening to Radio Londres or uttering de Gaulle's name.

They waited till they'd left the village to unfold the paper. It was a map, hastily sketched in violet ink, leading to the forest ranger's cabin, the place where your uncle had taken refuge before coming to Romaincourt. It was the group's first clandestine meeting place.

Gauthier belonged to Ceux de la Résistance (CDLR). His real name was Mayoux. He was born in Lyon but taught English in Nancy. I didn't hear anyone mention him till long after the war. If you recall, I was studying in Paris, and you've probably guessed that even if I'd been in Romaincourt, I wouldn't have heard anything either. Keep your mouth, your eyes, and your ears shut—that's what people around here did best. And for that matter, it was probably the best thing to do.

Today we know a little bit more about that enigmatic period of our beautiful, beloved Vosges. There are the archives. People who've got nothing to hide have talked. Those who fought, including your uncle, have now gained recognition—true, sixty years after the fact and after a great deal of difficulty—thanks to Pinéguette. They're mentioned on the steles, in public squares, in the alleys and streets, with words that prove they did not die in vain. One can't say as much for the others, doomed to shame, anonymity, contempt, everlasting mistrust. The others, the cowards, the ones who were resigned, who compromised—some of them had their heads shaved; others were hung or executed as the crowd looked on, booing and spitting. Some of those bastards are still around, bowing under the weight of their fear, skulking in the mire of their shame, forced to live under the accusing eye of their neighbors. Perhaps they aren't the ones, perhaps it was someone else. How are we to know? Their world is so petty, nothing is ever clear.

You went to Epinal, you visited Mount Virgin, you photographed the stele.

You read his name engraved there, next to that of Arbuger and many others. There were some sixty of them executed in that same place.

Now that you know how they met each other, I'll try and explain how they went about the task of resisting and how the Germans rounded them up.

You must have surmised that Mayoux was the London contact in Lorraine. His very first mission was to set up a Resistance group in the Vosges. For the people in London, these mountains held a lot of advantages: they are very near Switzerland; they're covered with dense forests that are an extension of those of the Haute-Marne; they can shelter innumerable clandestine paths; the *ballons* (rounded mountaintops) are of significant strategic interest and the rivers are easily forded; they're peopled with hardy and discreet peasants, accustomed to food shortages and to the cold, literally hardened by epidemics and wars.

Mayoux heard of Marcel Arbuger, who dragged Froitier into the picture because he was his friend, because there wasn't anyone else available. You see, Mister, what we so very solemnly call the "Resistance" today was still nothing but a joke, just a good laugh at the time. A few exalted young people would bang their fists on the table after several glasses of plum brandy, "Goddamn it! Let's put up a fight!"

They'd promise to set off a bomb at the Feldkommandantur, consider packing off to London, but then nothing more would come of it until the next binge. The country was on its knees, Mister. All people could do was improvise—it was a daily struggle just to survive. Some were capable of betraying their brother, deporting a friend to Germany for a ration ticket, for a couple of pounds of potatoes. There were the willing collaborators and there were the others, those who raged in silence, their feelings of helplessness and frustration gnawing at their insides, persuaded they should resist—fight, but unable to make up their minds how to go about it, convinced they needed arms, but not knowing where to find them. The people in London—nearly as lost as they were—knew those were the only people they could count on, if they could somehow be organized, prepared, and armed. Those people—just ordinary folks like you or I—who had never thought they would one day participate in a war, who'd never even dreamt of it, who abhorred it are today's heroes.

So Arbuger had probably never listened to Radio Londres but when the first sign was sent from Nancy, he answered yes without thinking twice. He believed it was necessary to put up a fight. Except he'd never fought before. He'd never held a firearm in his hands.

After an insane week of arbitrary meetings, interspersed with passwords and games of hide-and-seek, Arbuger found himself alone in his small apartment in Lamarche with the notorious bag sitting in a corner like a booby trap: excited, disconcerted by that fascinating, dangerous object that held both liberty and death.

His eyes lingered over the dog-eared corners, the cheap paper, the barely legible and poorly typed texts, the margins with carbon smears. Perhaps he was expecting to find the remedy for the unbearable anxiety that was beginning to tighten in his throat.

"Your mission is to create the first Resistance group in the Vosges."

He'd thought the task would be easier. He'd just been given a marvelous tool, but unfortunately they'd neglected to include the instructions for use along with it.

He sat there till the first twinkling of dawn, his thoughts interrupted by spells of drowsing. But when he went up to join his wife in bed, he knew that when he awoke, his life would never be the same again.

By that time, Addi Bâ was firmly rooted in the Vosges. He made his way around the region from farm to farm, from dairy to dairy, taking part in communions and funerals; by night he would secretly go out into hamlets—sometimes to see his partisans, other times his lovers. People welcomed him, knowing they should neither serve him pork nor alcohol for he was Muslim, nor plum syrup for he hated it. Above all, they knew he would ask them ridiculous questions about Chaumont—that was perhaps the only thing that occasioned people to doubt his mental stability. "No one can come out of such a catastrophe unscathed," they'd say as an excuse for him, evidently thinking of the Battle of the Meuse.

As I told you, as soon as the rumor that he was in Romaincourt started going around, Yolande Valdenaire began visiting him from time to time. But we never knew if it was her or her ghost, her silhouette seemed so ethereal, her footsteps so stealthy, and her disappearance so lightning quick. She'd appear like a glimmer over by the washhouse, melt in with the trunks of the trees and the walls for a few fractions of a second, then she'd slip into your uncle's house so noiselessly, one would have thought she'd gone through the wall instead of the door.

When it wasn't she who came to him, he would go out to meet her and we'd see them walking side by side, whispering something we imagined to be dangerous or reprehensible: at the train station in Merrey, at the fountain in Saint-André-les-Vosges, in the shade of the bushes on Sapinière ridge, and in this country—where every windowpane has some ten pairs of eyes—no one spoke of anything but that. What were they up to, what might they be planning together?

"The Resistance, of course! The Resistance!"

They had to pass arms, tracts, and messages right under the nose of the SS. They had to brave patrols and bad weather, meet up in the most unheard-of places, confide in strangers that could well be either informers or friends, give up leisure time and family life, risk the gallows or the gas chamber at any moment.... It was all downright crazy or impossible—it drained your energy, set your nerves on edge, but, all things considered, that particular type of resistance seemed less exhausting, less dangerous to them than the other kind they were secretly putting up to keep clear of the abyss....

The fact is, months had gone by since the Bois de Chenois, and a lot of things had changed. In Petit-Bourg, the feeling of impending calamity that had nagged at young Etienne was gaining ground every day. Though it hadn't yet reached the attic, it had gone far beyond the garden.

Hubert Valdenaire's health had taken a quite worrisome turn, and young Etienne was convinced that your uncle's arrival had something to do with it. Besides his damaged lungs, his phobia of war, there was now an additional unforeseen problem: jealousy. Morbid, hysteric jealousy, all the more intolerable since it was absolutely unfounded.

The behavior of that ordinarily gentle, loving husband grew to be nastier, more puzzling by the day. The unpleasant encounter he'd had on his way to pick mushrooms had awakened the fears he'd been attempting to suppress since 1918: old age, illness, going back to the trenches, and losing Yolande.

Of course, he ended up finding out that she'd put Addi Bâ up at the school in Saint-André-les-Vosges and that she was visiting him secretly in Romaincourt. Thus, their conversations often sounded like arguments.

This is what young Etienne heard one evening when he put his ear to the floorboards, as he'd gotten in the habit of doing since your uncle arrived.

"He'll be the end of you. He'll bring nothing good to you or me or anyone else. Nothing but blood, nothing but quarrels and conflict! Look what he's done to us, Yolande, just look!"

"This is war, Hubert! It's burning him up inside just like it is everyone else."

"You love him, don't you?"

"Like a son! Like Etienne!"

"Yolande, look at me straight in the face and tell me the truth!"

Yolande was telling the truth, an ambiguous, complex truth, but the truth all the same, one that she wasn't able to see all the facets of herself.

He called her "Mama" and she called him "Son". It had begun effortlessly, naturally. And that naturalness was precisely what was ruining Hubert's and Etienne's life, what was consuming them, with an inextinguishable flame, because it was hidden, hidden and impossible to confess.

Yolande was still very beautiful even though she was past forty. She thrived on all the ideals that young people espouse, whereas her husband had lung problems, intestinal and arterial problems as well, but he mostly had stomach problems—he had no stomach for anger or indignation, no stomach for fighting any longer.

Addi had the vitality and charm of a movie star: he had no control over his desire to charm, was unable to quell the wild and confused longings that came over him whenever a beautiful woman walked by. Between those two, Mister, it just couldn't have been a simple relationship.

Young Etienne sometimes spoke to me about the hostile atmosphere that pervaded his parents' house, but he'd mention it in such elusive terms, I felt I knew even less after having listened to him.

Marcel Arbuger was aware that school got out at five o'clock and that, after having closed up the classroom and padlocked the gate, the schoolmistress would jump on her bicycle, steer around the fountain, take the road to Petit-Bourg, and cover the three kilometers between the school and her house. He waited for her out in the countryside, lurking behind an elderberry bush. When he caught sight of her at the top of the slope, he came out in the open and started waving his arms. She wanted to ride past without stopping, but changed her mind at the last minute when she saw the man frantically hailing her down and coming dangerously close.

"It's you? Are you crazy? Right out in broad daylight?"

"Excuse me, Yolande Valdenaire, but..."

"I'm afraid you're mistaken—my name isn't Yolande Valdenaire."

"I'm sorry, Aunt Armelle!"

"Dear God! What do you want? Tell me quick and get out of here!"

"The people in London... I mean the people in Nancy, they've asked me... to come straight to the point. I need to talk to you about the Resistance—"

She cut him off with a quick dry laugh. "The Resistance! And you're the person they've sent to talk to me about the Resistance?"

"Me, you, everyone! But we mustn't stay here—there are ears everywhere, and the Jerries could come by any minute."

She slowly looked him over from head to toe, trying to figure out if she should bawl him out or feel sorry for the people in Nancy and London.

She let out a sigh and said, "Follow me."

She took him to the small apartment where she'd hidden your uncle two years earlier.

"Sit down, try to remain calm, and tell me what you want to tell me."

"It's what everyone is dreaming about, Mrs. Valdenaire, working with London. Just go out into the countryside, you'll see, all the young people dream only of that. Except... distributing leaflets, tearing down swastikas, derailing trains isn't all that effective, and the young men have grown weary of it.... Finally, London has come up with a good idea.... At last they understand that it's time to take action, if you know what I mean..."

"Go on."

"Well... they want us to create a Resistance group, a Maquis, right here in the Vosges. Except we don't have any idea how to go about it.... You were in the First World War..."

And his eyes were brimming with hope as if her response could erase all of the wrongs that made his life miserable.

"Your husband as well!" he hurriedly added, believing that it would help to convince her.

"Leave my husband out of this!"

"Very well, then, the other guy."

"Who?"

"The black man!"

"The black man's got a name!"

"You know, the Tirailleur! He's the only one of us who has any experience with firearms. And what's more, he's on our side: he's always talked about taking up arms, and the farmers like him too! And you have a lot of influence over him."

"And what kind of a Resistance group do these people from London… sorry, from Nancy, want to create?"

"They want it to be centered here in the township of Lamarche to make ready for the Allied invasion scheduled in May 1943. There's no dearth of thick forest and isolated farms."

"We'll need soldiers and arms to operate a Resistance group."

"That's why I mentioned the Tirailleur."

"Okay. He won't object to the idea. But dear God, please obey orders! What did we say in the hunter's cabin? A maximum of two contacts for each of us: one above, one below. Now leave and, I beg of you, find some other way of operating."

Everyone knows your uncle's wildest dream was to go to London. He'd talked about it one evening at the Soulaucourt dairy farm. After having listened to the radio at my parents' house so often, he'd ended up persuading himself that all was not lost, that the people in London weren't just poor Utopians, that they might bring about the resurrection of the homeland. Thus, when Yolande spoke to him about creating a Resistance group, he took her in his arms and gave her a big long kiss.

"That's wonderful news, Mama! The best I've heard since Neufchâteau!"

"You'll be in command! But we'll need fighting men and arms."

"The fighting men will be easy: we'll get them from the STO (Service du Travail Obligatoire or Compulsory Work Service). They'll see a double advantage in it: first of all, they'll be escaping the German tyranny and, secondly, we'll be offering them the opportunity to do what they've all been dreaming of doing: defending themselves. As for the arms, all we'll have to do is stoop down and pick them up. There are firearms hidden in every forest around here and, better yet, they're our very own; they once belonged to the French army."

"Yes, that's right, Son! Please try and stay put for a little while, if you see what I'm getting at: you could be contacted very soon. Come on, give me a kiss. I've got to go now!"

The network set to work very rapidly. Groups of three or four were stationed, preferably in isolated dairies and farms where the Jerries very rarely set foot, where the gendarmerie alone came by making the rounds every once in a while. What role did they play? That of dissuading parents from sending their children to Germany and helping the young men to escape by any means possible. They were then to go into training and prepare themselves for the invasion while keeping up the routine of turning out leaflets and distributing them, protecting escapees, Haguenaux (or Alsatians), and Jews.

The Resistance was made up of people like you and I, farmers, moonshine makers, poachers, schoolteachers, cheap restaurant owners, doctors, laundry women.

They weren't heroes, Mister, they were simply desperate!

Winter comes once a year; war comes twice every hundred years. The true enemy of the Vosges, Mister, was the croup. The Prussians and the cold could have been considered allies next to that blasted ailment. Go visit our cemeteries: you'll see that half of our dead succumbed to its assaults.

Take Madeline Arbuger, for example, my father's first wife. Marcel is a cousin of mine, Mister. He used to come around sometimes to have a little chat with Papa and drink some moonshine. Several times he ran into the Sergeant (that was after their mysterious meeting on the steps of the church) sitting in our parlor, always with one ear glued to the radio, glassy-eyed with the absent look of a starry-eyed daydreamer. Before that, he'd heard about the strange black man—in the mills and dairies, on the farms—the man who refused to accept the debacle and dreamt of going to London. A foreigner who came from the forests of Africa, who wanted to continue fighting when the white men had thrown down their arms and made a deal with the enemy. I watched them shake hands, exchange a few words about the weather, the constant radio blackouts, about the cryptic and fanciful messages the people in London enjoyed diffusing—people who were far from having to flee southward, far from the shortages, far from the deadly boot of the SS. I didn't have any idea that they'd been conniving together for quite some time and that the good Lord had mingled their destinies from the very beginning and determined that a year later they would die at the hands of the same firing squad.

Now that Marcel had met a member of the London group, now that—unbeknownst to his wife—he was keeping a bag full of tracts stashed away in his attic, you can understand why he needed to find a place where they could talk. One doesn't bring up subjects like that just anywhere. Papa was a known anti-Vichyiste; Mama was as silent as the grave; Mâmiche—who was afraid of everything—never got mixed up in things that were none of her business, but you never knew.

One day Marcel Arbuger came to see us and sat in the parlor for a long time, smoking one cigarette after another and pacing about nervously. When he believed I'd gone out into the garden, I heard him ask my father, "Where on earth can the Tirailleur be?"

"Undoubtedly over at Mâmiche's, chatting or embroidering!"

I could sense that Marcel was in a hurry to see him, needed to tell him something of grave importance that no one else knew about, not even Mâmiche, not even the Colonel.

Marcel was aware that even in the middle of the Vosges, your uncle had held on to those strange African customs of his. After having breakfast, he would meticulously rinse out his mouth, then fill a pot with water and disappear into the woods. It took Mâmiche—who was the first to notice this strange behavior—quite some time before deciding to confide her misgivings to my parents.

"That's what they do over there—they give thanks to the gods as soon as they've finished eating," answered my father in a knowing tone of voice.

Of course, that explanation was not entirely satisfactory.

"But what could he be doing with a pot full of water in the middle of the woods?" wondered all of Romaincourt.

Only recently was I able to resolve that enigma, following a journey to India organized by the episcopate. He was simply attending to the call of nature in the manner that people in those countries do.

Just picture Marcel, crouching under the pine trees, cackling in stupefaction upon seeing that! Just picture your uncle's reaction: "What in the world are you doing here? You weren't watching me, were you?"

"No, don't worry, I was completely distracted by those two roe deer mating over there."

"Yeah," your uncle chuckled in turn. "They say they only do it once a year, during mating season."

"They're very chaste. I know some folks who would be truly put out being a roe deer."

"Hey! It's not enough for you to come and disturb me in my privy, now you're sticking your nose into my night life? Careful, don't get me stirred up!"

"Marcel sensed the timing was just right. He joined your uncle discreetly in the woods before he'd finish buckling his belt.

"The Boène farm is with us. They'll be waiting for you tomorrow around midnight. Do you know where it is?"

"Uh, yes."

Then they talked about passwords, supplies, secret places for their meetings, about being cautious and discreet.

Your uncle had been to the Boène farm a few times to get milk. A modest property, quite a bit closer to Creuchot Forest than to the fields of La Villotte and difficult to see from the road because of the elderberry bushes and chestnut trees. He knew that Gaston Houillon was a good man and head of a family of four who were every bit as hardworking and humble as he was: his wife, Andrée; his son, Albert; and his daughters, Paulette and Jeannine. He knew that Marcel, who'd often worked for him as a tinsmith, would never get him mixed up with a *haltata* (that's what people from the Vosges call a crackpot). You could tell from Gaston's face, from the way he ran his farm, that he could be trusted beyond the shadow of a doubt.

"Thank you for working with us, Gaston! The Partisans' Oak! What a brilliant idea! So you'll be our sentinel. I know that the Germans will never get past a man like you."

"Just look at how vast the barn is!"

"The size of a dormitory, Gaston! Could we go up and visit your Partisans' Oak?"

"You're kidding, Sergeant! It's way out in the backwoods. You'd think there were two forests nestling one inside the other, hard to find, even in broad daylight. Tomorrow at dawn, get on your bicycle as usual, and you'll see my kids taking the cows up. When you're well out of sight, my son will take you to it. You'll see, you could camp there till the end of the war. They already used the place back in 1634 against Louis XIII's soldiers and again in 1870 against the Prussians."

"Wonderful, Gaston, just wonderful! I won't waste any more of your time. I'll be here waiting quietly in the underbrush for your children to go by."

— § —

It was a clearing as large as two football fields, surrounded by a crown of birch trees so dense and leafy it looked like a quickset hedge. Gaston was right. Your uncle glanced around the open space looking satisfied and mumbled inaudibly, "The Germans would have to be led here by one of the Resistance fighters in order to find this place. We'll be able to put up two hundred, maybe even three hundred men here. And three hundred is nearly an army already!"

Then he turned toward the boy. "If I asked you to join us, would you do it, Albert?"

"Well, it's just that I need to help with the farm. My parents can't get by on their own with only my two little sisters."

"You misunderstood me, Albert, I'm not talking about the camp—I'm talking about the Jerries."

"Well, as far as I'm concerned, I don't like the Jerries either, and I can speak for everyone at the Boène."

"What could you do, Albert?"

"Well, a part from taking the livestock to the pastures..."

"Perfect, Albert, I'll promise you lots of livestock to take out to pasture!"

He went to meet Marcel Arbuger (alias Simon) in the agreed-upon place and, with all the enthusiasm of a kid who'd just won a game of ninepins, told him, "If your Vercingetorix had known of a place like that, the Gauls would have colonized the Romans. ... All right, we've found the arena; now all we need are the gladiators."

"My contacts haven't been loafing. In the Youth Work Camp in Méricourt, there are almost ten of them ready to pack their bags."

"No kidding! We could send out scouts to get them tonight or tomorrow."

"Impossible! There are Jerries all over the place! An act of sabotage was committed at the train station in Granges-sur-Vologne. They're a bit nervous for the time being. Especially after those young people were arrested in Vittel for illegally wearing the Star of David and all the agitation about the incarceration of ninety-nine communists in Saint-Dié...."

"At least it's proof they're not welcome. What more does Vichy need to get that through its head?"

"Our radio is in London. We don't care about Vichy... okay? We'll wait for things to calm down, and then we'll get our boys in the youth camp moving. A camp with no fighters is dreary."

"The camp doesn't have fighters yet, but I've found a name for it."

"What?"

"Camp Deliverance!

Oh-ho! Camp Deliverance! That's almost as good as Lamartine!"

— § —

The next day while attempting to meet up with his mama in the Bois de Chenois, he realized Marcel hadn't been talking nonsense. There were Jerries all over the place, not only at intersections and train stations. He turned back, taking grassy paths that wound between the trees known only to him, to poachers, and to the deer.

He lay low for a few days in Romaincourt, where he did some cooking at Mâmiche's place again, listened to the radio at our house, went to play checkers at the Colonel's, or cut wood at the schoolteacher's. I remember all that. It was during the fall break and I'd come to spend a few days with my parents.

One evening, as we were sitting in front of our leek soup and listening to the radio, London suddenly cut off the music to stick one of those phrases into their programs that was only comprehensible to initiates: "The rooster will eat the hazelnuts."

Once again, just like the last time, he pushed his bowl of soup away, raised a hand to motion good-bye, and disappeared into the night. I didn't understand why until much later, thanks to Colonel Melun's explanations. An English plane coming back from a reconnaissance mission in Italy had been shot down over the Bois de Chenois. Your uncle, Arbuger, and the mayor succeeded in recuperating the pilot and smuggling him into Switzerland right under the Germans' noses.

At that time, a lot of unusual, disconnected things were happening in Romaincourt that I wouldn't understand the meaning of, or the way they fit together, until a long time after the war.

For example, I remember that strange evening when, after dinner, Papa abruptly announced, "You'll go spend the night at Totor's!"

"At Totor's?"

Seeing his discomfiture, Mama had come to his aid.

"Uh... we heard that there's beef over in Bourbonne-les-Bains... and, well, we're going to try and get some."

"At this time in the evening?"

"Well, yes... That's what contraband is all about!"

At noon, although your uncle customarily came to eat with us, Mama took the meal over to his place. With two plates and napkins.

Two or three days later, a group of Germans armed to the teeth rode up on motorcycles, in jeeps, and in trucks. They came rushing over to our house and pulled my father outside with a revolver to his head. Guttural-sounding words were shouted out left and right, and in all those filthy mouths, one phrase was repeated like a leitmotif: "*Der schwarze Terrorist!* The black terrorist!"

They pushed my father over in the direction of your uncle's house. I heard the sound of a door being busted in and that of dishes being broken. Boots thundered up the worm-eaten staircase leading to the barn. A few seconds went by and then the floor of the barn fell through, and, for an instant, we thought the war had come to Romaincourt. One of the Jerries had his buttocks cut when he fell on the reaper. I never would have understood any of that if it weren't for the letter that came from South Africa three years ago, following an article by Colonel Melun that was published in a Parisian newspaper. It was written by a man named Horn who was none other than our notorious English aviator. The letter was filled with praise for your uncle and related in minute detail his plane being shot down and his epic journey to Switzerland.

So, after having parachuted out of the plane, Horn had been taken in by an old woman on a farm where your uncle and the mayor came to get him. How? We'll probably never know.

One thing for certain is that they must have traveled thirty kilometers each way in the dark. They probably took turns having the pilot ride on the back of their bikes. They went through the village without arousing suspicion and then hid him in the barn under the hay. Another thing for sure is that Papa and Mama were in on the plan and that Papa had led the German officer toward the rotten part of the barn on purpose.

The Germans panicked at the sight of the SS's buttocks literally cut in two. They quickly realized he couldn't be transported, given the quantity of blood gushing from his wound. They left two men to watch over him and went speeding off toward Vittel with their sirens howling full blast to bring back a doctor and an ambulance. As a result, they ended up forgetting the reason they'd come and left with the wounded man, who died that same night.

The Englishman would also explain to us that his passage into Switzerland had not been achieved as rapidly as we first thought. It was a long procedure that lasted three months, during which he was moved around from farm to farm, from village to village, from one person to another, often changing itineraries and identities.

I also remember that when I was leaving to go back to Paris at the end of the holiday, Addi Bâ came to see me the day before my departure.

"Don't forget to come by to get my onions!"

There were exactly ten onions, just like the other times. Ten onions for an entire mosque! Still another enigma that I wouldn't resolve until long after the war ended. Reading a magazine two years after the Liberation, I learned that onions were one of the principle channels of communications for the Resistance. It was quite simple: one just wrote his message on cigarette paper and then slipped it between the layers of peeling. But that wasn't the only trick. People also pretended to be trading cheese or hams with hidden messages that could easily have had their receiver sent to the firing squad or to a concentration camp.

At Moulin Froid, where your uncle often used to go, there lived a woman and her seventeen-year-old son, whose father was a prisoner of war—interned in a German camp near the Polish border. Your uncle had immediately noticed that strong, intelligent boy and knew he would make use of him one day.

He came to get him one evening and led him over to the manure pit to have a man-to-man talk with him.

"It's time for you to commit, Bertrand! Do what it takes to make your father proud of you when he comes back from Germany."

"But I have to help Mama with the farm."

"We're at war, Bertrand—the farm isn't enough anymore. Your father and a bunch of other brave people are in Germany, and their lives are in constant danger. It's our duty to risk our lives too."

"If the war were still on, I would have enlisted."

"Ah, that's the kind of talk I like to hear! Are you familiar with Méricourt, Bertrand?"

"Sure I am—it's my mother's village."

"Have you heard of the youth camp? Do you know how to get there?"

"When I was little, we used to play ninepins there."

"Good. Tomorrow we'll meet there at midnight… not at the camp itself but in the trees overlooking the buildings."

Bertrand was a bit disappointed not to find anything exciting about "Operation Youth 43," the very first Resistance mission carried out by Camp Deliverance. He met up with Addi Bâ in the stand of trees as planned. Your uncle took out a flashlight and sent signals in the direction of one of the buildings. A shadow slipped out, moved along the length of the courtyard, crossed the bed of roses, and hopped over the wall. Then another did the same, and the scene was repeated twelve times. The boys crossed the street, made their way along the walls of the silo, and, crouching, quickly entered the woods. It was so simple that your uncle felt he needed to murmur something so they wouldn't feel let down.

"This is only the beginning—wait till you see what comes next."

The dense vegetation and the moonless, snowless night made it necessary for the boys to walk one behind the other, holding a length of string that Addi Bâ had luckily thought to bring along to keep from getting lost. They walked for three long hours, circumventing main roads and houses, avoiding patrols and barking dogs.

Addi took out his torch again when they drew near to the Boène farm. He sent a signal, and Paul came to open the gate.

Your uncle quickly understood that he had to target his partisans very precisely. Not just anyone could live that kind of life. Young men with no profession, no family responsibilities were needed. Boys who were sufficiently hostile toward the enemy, boys for whom the Resistance meant a chance of escaping the Youth Work Camps and the STO.

When they were inside the hangar, Addi Bâ locked the door securely before taking out his flashlight again. They were very young peasant boys as he was accustomed to seeing during his wanderings. He scrutinized them one by one in the harsh light and guessed that the youngest one was going on sixteen and the oldest one wasn't yet twenty-five. At the sight of those faces, most of which still had red acne marks, he was overwhelmed with a feeling of anger mingled with compassion. He shook his head to ward it off, telling himself, "War knows no age. Tough luck, young men, you just weren't born at the right time."

He switched off the flashlight and spoke into the darkness as would an executioner or a confessor.

"Is there anyone among you who regrets being here?"

When no one answered, he continued, "Very well, then. You are now men, and I will treat you as such until given proof to the contrary."

"You spoke to us of the Resistance!"

He switched the light back on nervously.

"Who said that?"

It was a tall boy with frizzy hair, the kind who likes to show off. A little while ago, in the woods, he hadn't stopped whispering despite the orders he'd been given.

"What's your name, young man?"

"Armand! Armand Demange, Mister!"

"Sergeant Major or Sir! Listen to me, Armand Demange, the Resistance isn't in the woods; it's in the mind. Get it into your minds that you are soldiers! Get it into your minds that you are underground! And after that, shut up, close your eyes, and do what you're told to do. Got that, Armand Demange?"

"Yes, boss!"

"Sergeant Major! Sergeant Major Addi Bâ!"

He turned off the flashlight again, feeling guilty about having shouted so sternly.

"That'll be all for tonight. I'll stop by to get you tomorrow after the cows have been milked and take you up there. And it will be the same routine every day."

He turned the flashlight back on to make sure no one had asked any questions.

"Every day until we've built barracks up there. Until *you*—and everyone who joins you in the coming weeks—have built barracks. In the meantime, no talking, no going out to urinate. They're in your hands now, Bertrand! You're in command when I'm not around. They are to strictly obey your every order. Got that, Armand Demange?"

"Got it, sir!"

It was spring. After the snowdrifts, the sudden March downpours came to rough up the Vosgian countryside: disfiguring buildings, making rivers rage, covering the streets and plains with a thick layer of mud. Our young recruits cleared the land and began to pile up wood, bricks, and stones. The first contingent freed from the clutches of the STO arrived when the foundations of the first barracks were being laid.

I need to explain to you what the STO was. I'm not certain you heard about that strange entity all the way across the seas over there on the banks of the Limpopo. In the spring of 1942, the war took a different turn. It was no longer a question of conquering France—that had already been accomplished—but of exploiting it to enrich the occupier, taking their payment in kind, in a manner of speaking. The decision was made to send three hundred fifty thousand French laborers to Germany. The first year they simply encouraged volunteers with propaganda campaigns, then Vichy made it obligatory in 1943.

At the Partisans' Oak, the Resistance group was still in its early stages. On the outside, the network that had been patiently put into place was already functional. They simply needed to multiply their contacts, improve the message system, and speed up recruitment. However, in Méricourt there simply were no more volunteers, and, besides, the Germans would end up suspecting something. Addi Bâ decided to meet with Simon to talk things over.

Slouching on a bench in the public square in Lamarche, head raised as if he were observing the clouds, Addi Bâ sensed someone sit down on the bench behind him, heard the man pronounce the password and begin talking in a low voice as if he were reading the paper. Your uncle assumed that Simon was in Nancy—probably to receive orders—and the man called Alex had been sent in his place. Back in London, things were beginning to gather speed. The landings would be taking place soon—next May—that was set now. It was time for the people in the Vosges to get their asses moving.

The underground had finally finished setting up its network in Epinal, in Contrexéville, all the way out into the remotest hamlets. Now it was time to concentrate on the Resistance fighters, give them the means of carrying out missions before spring came to an end. The people from up high had accepted his idea of forgetting about the youth camps and turning toward the STO instead. Many more men could be recruited there, and maneuvering was less risky. There were STO conscripts everywhere, and they needed to move around a lot, take carts, bicycles, trains to get to Germany. Therefore the Resistance had many opportunities to act, whereas the youth camps were set up in veritable barracks in only a few locations.

Perceiving that the man was preparing to leave after having folded his newspaper, your uncle asked in a worried tone of voice, "So what about the toys? When will we get the toys?"

"Gauthier sends his regards! Let the boys grow up a little first—they'll get the toys later! And don't worry, as far as his health is concerned, everything is fine. Aunt Armelle can vouch for that."

"What is Simon going to do?"

"It's his job to pick golden chanterelles! And yours to cook them!"

That meant the tasks had been assigned once and for all. Simon would drive the game back toward the Boène farm, and Addi Bâ would lead them up to the Partisans' Oak, where he was to take care of feeding and training them. Simon, the politician; he, the military man. Each had his responsibility and would not encroach upon that of the other.

The following week, the Germans called for all young men born between 1920 and 1922 to undergo examinations in La Villotte, and Dr. Couillaud was in charge. He declared a good number of them unfit for service. The others pretended to head for Germany, getting on the train at the station in Merrey. But they took advantage of the general confusion to get off in Contrexéville. From there they walked through the forest till they reached Lamarche, where Simon was waiting for them. The next morning Addi Bâ had only to pick them up in Old Man Gaston's barn and take them up to the Partisans' Oak to join their predecessors.

At the end of April, there were already more than eighty boys at the camp. Using stones, branches, and wooden disks recuperated from the local sawmills, they erected two makeshift barracks with little shacks all around them that oddly resembled African huts.

During the day, your uncle taught them basic military skills; by night, he scoured the surrounding territory looking for food. He would go to a cattle breeder and say, "Slit that calf's throat—it'll be for the Resistance!"

He did the same with millers or farmers. On his way back, his bicycle would be loaded with sacks of flour, cheese, and vegetables. Sometimes the donor brought his contribution to the Boène farm himself, or sometimes a few recruits were appointed to go and pick up the supplies.

Addi enjoyed catching them playing cards or dressed up as wild Africans with paint on their faces and belts of leaves around their hips. They expected him to be offended or hurt by their antics, but he wasn't. They were almost disappointed, not really knowing themselves if they did it to wile away the time or to put him to the test. They would stand at attention as soon as they saw him coming.

"Go recuperate the firearms instead of acting like smart alecks."

After losing the Battle of the Meuse, the French army had lost its head, both literally and figuratively. The soldiers had thrown their rifles and uniforms down on the roads, stolen bicycles from the stores to accelerate their flight. Three years later, the Germans and the partisans were still vying over that important arsenal. I already told you that the Germans had created a battalion of Malagasies and Africans in Epinal, which they used exclusively for collecting war booty. As far as the Resistance was concerned, they found that getting hold of the abandoned arms had a double advantage: it kept them out of the Germans' hands, while arming their fighters at the same time. The operations would always take place at the crack of dawn or at nightfall. Addi Bâ would send them out in small groups along the roads or following streams. He left it up to Bertrand to supervise the disassembling and upkeep of their acquisitions.

On that particular day, they were playing neither ninepins nor cards nor Zulus nor charades. Addi Bâ found them in the middle of a scene that took him a good ten minutes to comprehend. They had set up a makeshift altar that was remindful of the church in Romaincourt. One of them, wearing a false beard and a monk's robe, was baptizing a novice and singing bawdy songs that the others—draped in moth-eaten sheets—chimed in with. They were all so absorbed in their little pantomime that they didn't hear their commander arrive.

They didn't realize he was there until he began to snarl, "What's going on here?"

The group broke up, and each of the boys hurried away and disappeared into his particular barracks or hut.

"Everyone get out here on the double before I set fire to this camp!"

They came back out, laughing in stitches, feeling as ashamed of their silly shenanigans as they were amused.

"Who organized this?"

The shadow of the monk finally appeared in the door of one of the shacks.

"Step forward... Take off that beard..."

The culprit took off his disguise, and Addi was hardly surprised to recognize Armand Demange, the troublemaker.

"I knew it must be you! All right, you're on mess duty now!"

When the meal was ready, your uncle snatched the plate from Armand's hands.

"No grub for you tonight! Go get dressed and don't forget to put on a sweater and some good shoes."

He held out a sheet of paper.

"Look closely, the red mark shows the location of an abandoned machine gun on Mouzon Plain. You just have to follow the arrows. Here, take the flashlight. As soon as it's dark, you'll go out and get it. The camp won't hit the sack until you've finished disassembling and reassembling it without error. Walking up here a little while ago, I was wondering who I might assign this chore to. Your childish pranks have decidedly relieved me of the dilemma."

It would take an hour to walk down there and just as long to come back, that is, if you had your hands free. When Armand set out, an icy gloom fell over the camp. Recriminating glances converged on the commander. No one dared say a word until Armand came back, but it was easy to read their thoughts: *For something that trivial? And why him, on such a dark night? He's been gone for three hours already. What if he's been captured by a patrol? What if he ran into a pack of wolves?*

It took Armand four hours to get back. His being late even lent an uneasy glimmer to the commander's eyes; pride was the only thing that kept him from sending scouts out to see what had happened. To his great relief, Armand finally reappeared. Exhausted, he laid his bundle on the ground, took off his sweater, and, meticulously—but with tight-clenched jaws—disassembled the mechanism part by part and reassembled it without fault. After that, he stood up and went into his shack holding back his sobs.

"It's not fair, sir, I swear it's not fair!"

The incident was quickly forgotten, buried under the multitude of events that governed life in the camp: the bad weather, the exercises, the feats one had to accomplish to find food, the incessant arrival of new recruits, most of which had escaped from trains to avoid the STO.

But not a week went by that Armand was not punished once again, for having slapped a comrade or refused to peel potatoes—no one really knew exactly why. Should there be no more matches, he'd be sent out to the Boène farm. For the next stupid thing he did, he had to go out and gather ten faggots of wood before sunset. Ten minutes later he was back, not toting a faggot of wood but a flesh-and-blood human being with hands and feet tied whom he laid at the commander's feet.

"I caught him spying on us. I don't like traitors."

"Now what have you gone and done, Armand Demange?"

"He's a collaborator! I get to execute him!"

Your uncle pushed him away, untied the victim, and recognized Celestin.

"Oh no! My God, no!"

"I came to enlist," whimpered the young boy.

"Enlist! Does your mother know you're here?"

"I didn't have time to tell her."

"Then, you and I are going to pay her a little visit."

He straddled his bicycle and had Celestin sit on the baggage rack. However, before taking off, he turned toward his troops.

"Bertrand, you're in charge. Wood-gathering duty is canceled."

— § —

Huguette was busy at the counter, oblivious to the grumblings of two or three *cheûlard*-boozers sipping their moonshine. The proprietress showed no surprise at seeing Addi and the boy come in.

"Guess what brings me here, Huguette!"
"You've come to say hello, what else?"
"With your son?"
"Is something wrong?"
"It'd be best if you explain," he said, pulling Celestin over to the counter.
"That's fine with me, but I don't know where to start."
"Huguette, you shouldn't let your child hang out when there's a war on."
"Hang out? Poor kid, he got up at dawn to light the oven, knead the dough, and cook the first batches of bread, like a man. Then he helped me with the bar until around two in the afternoon. I had to give him a bit of a breather!"
"He came to see me up there, he wants to join."
"Ho-ho! You're not going to fall for that, Addi! Even five-year-old kids say that. 'I want to join the Resistance.' It's just make-believe, they play at being Resistance fighters, like kids play cowboys.... You know very well you can't do that, my little Celestin. Mama needs you here, the café, the bakery, the vegetable garden—there's too much to do! And your foot couldn't even lift an army boot. You'll have to wait for the next war, little Celestin, the next one. If this one ever ends."
"Well, now that this little misunderstanding has been cleared up, I'll bid you both good night, I've had a hard day."
"Without having a chicory *aouatte*?"
"No thanks, Huguette, no thanks."
She stepped quickly over to join him as he was opening the door.
"Someone talked to me about a scheme for getting some lamb. Come see me tomorrow."
"Right, I'll stop by at noon for my *frichti*."

— § —

He was just finishing up his *frichti*, which consisted of a sandwich stuffed with sardines, tomatoes, and onions, when a gendarme came in after knocking heavily at the door.

"Huguette Lambert? I have orders to speak with you, Madame."

"Go ahead!"

"Not in front of all these people, Madame. It's confidential."

"Do you mean to say I should have you come up to my place?"

"If that is the only way to speak to you in private."

Busy with his meal and his glass of lemonade, Addi heard them go up the stairs. Suddenly a wild, pained cry shook the walls as the gendarme came bounding down the steps four at a time like a thief.

Addi jumped up but was preceded by Celestin. When he reached the top of the stairs, he found the mother and her son hugging one another, shaken with sobs, looking at each other with red eyes but unable to say a word.

"What's going on? Tell me!"

He repeated the question several times to no avail. That's when he noticed the various objects—harbingers of tragedy—scattered on the coffee table in front of the sofa where Huguette and Celestin were slumped: a watch, a lighter, something that looked like a notebook or an agenda, and, next to it all, a paper written in black ink by the hand of one of those calligraphers who are paid to make the slightest administrative missive ominous and repulsive.

He took the paper and read it as she let go of her son for a minute to turn toward him with a reproachful look.

"I told you he would never see his son, I told you so. But you didn't believe me..."

"By the way, where is your child?"

"In Roncourt, with his grandparents. They take care of him from time to time to let me have a rest."

"Huguette, I never asked you what you named him."

"Firmin, like his father, Firmin Lambert!"

He was standing in the middle of the room, not knowing what to say or do, what excuse to bring up to be able to leave the place. The anxious cries coming from the bar brought him back to reality.

As he came down, he said, in a tone of voice that he tried to make as neutral as possible, "Take care of her, please!"

And he hurriedly jumped on his bike.

— § —

For two days he didn't dare go back, two days that he devoted to his secret meetings with Simon and Yolande, as if the news he'd just learned had cut the ties that bound him to Huguette, to Celestin, and to the camp. And when he finally made up his mind to go there, all along the way he was beset with the thought that the bereaved widow would blame the unbearable tragedy on him and that the red, grief-stricken eyes of the orphan, would avoid his.

The leaden shroud of mourning had snuffed out the lights, bolted shut the doors of the premises that would now house but the monologues of *cheûlards*, the stooped form of a woman doomed to spend her life shrouded in black. He knocked for a long time before young Celestin came to open the door. He was expecting the same scene as the other day: they would still be sprawled on the bed weeping, blaming the pain that was too excruciating to bear alone on others. The objects that had come back from Germany were still there, scattered about on the coffee table. But the tenants had changed places. Dry-eyed and even with a faint smile on their lips, they were busying themselves at the other end of the apartment where he joined them. It was as if suddenly they had rid themselves of all of the resentment the good Lord had vested them with.

"Let's go into the parlor, Addi, I'll make you some coffee, real coffee. I got some yesterday along with a leg of lamb."

Life had begun anew for them, and then that blasted gendarme had come through the door of that house bringing grief.

She went to make the coffee, while Celestin, who'd remained in the other room, was noisily putting boxes away. He took the opportunity to read the paper again. Death due to tuberculosis. Tuberculosis! Not of hunger, not of cold, not from a bullet in his head, from tuberculosis! He hadn't noticed that detail the last time.

She served him the coffee and pointed to the porcelain cup, murmuring without the slightest hint of bitterness, "He drank his last cup of coffee in a cup just like that."

"I have to go, Huguette. It's comforting to see that you're both holding up," he said just as Celestin came into the room. "Perfect timing."

Suddenly, Huguette hurried over to the coffee table and picked up the watch, which she fastened around her son's wrist. Then she took his hand and placed it in Addi's.

"Take him into the woods, take him wherever you want!"

"You've gone mad, Huguette! His place is here at his mother's side!"

"Until that letter arrived. Things have changed now. He's right, his place is up there with you."

"At his age!"

"He spends his days killing Germans in the garden with his water pistol."

"Not now, Huguette!"

"Why?"

"Um, let's give him a chance to get over his grief!"

Turning to Celestin, he said, "Here, take this pistol—it's a real one! I'll give you the bullets when you've finished growing up. You don't kill Germans with water pistols."

He went out without looking back.

— § —

It was around that same time that Yolande, alias Aunt Armelle, came into contact with the receiving center in Epinal—that was where the war prisoners who worked outside the camps came to eat at noon. The director had obtained some stamps that made it possible to establish false certificates of liberated prisoners; she also had SNCF (French National Railway Company) armbands that allowed people to circulate between the gray zone and the occupied zone. Let me explain, Mister. See the occupiers had split France up into three zones, three pieces of pie, to use Nonon Totor's expression: the occupied zone in the North, the free zone in the South, and here in the East, a gray zone that was to be Germanized.

Armed with those false papers, your uncle left the camp in Bertrand's hands for several days and made his way to Paris. Yes, Paris, I'm sure of what I'm saying because young Etienne had me read the missive with the mosque's letterhead that he sent to his mother. What he went to do in Paris, no one will ever know. Especially since that letter was more like a secret code than a true piece of correspondence.

Just listen to it:

> *Dear Mama,*
>
> *I've arrived safely. The celebration is on the 11th, not on Sunday.*
>
> *I saw my friends Saleh and Abdallah, we had a warm reunion. The bags are late. I believe I'll receive them tomorrow.*
>
> *I've got to go now.*
>
> *Here's wishing you a very good day,*
>
> *Your beloved son.*

He came to Paris without trying to see me, without even phoning me!

Soon after that, I recall I was on holiday in Romaincourt again and—after the onions—I had still another opportunity to witness a peculiar incident that would not become clear until after the war. On that particular day, Addi Bâ was sitting in front of his door and waiting for me to come out on my way to catch the train. I waved good-bye to him and turned left on the road leading to the Merrey train station.

"Not that way, Germaine, the other way!"

"But..."

"Do as I say, Germaine!"

He had uttered those words in such an intimidating voice, something told me I should obey without asking any questions.

I left the village and walked along the edge of the forest humming a tune. And guess what happened then? A monster leapt out of the underbrush, nearly knocking me over. Horrified, I closed my eyes, believing my last hour had come, but when I opened them again, a puny young boy with tousled hair was standing before me.

"What are you doing here?" I said in a quavering voice that made him laugh.

"I'm your brother."

"I've never had a brother."

"Here, these are my papers!"

His name was Tergoresse, all right, Antoine Tergoresse, born May 5th in Romaincourt, to Leon and Adelaïde Tergoresse. He was my brother.

I turned my back and stepped up my pace so he would understand I didn't want to have anything to do with him. But he was stubborn and ran as fast as I did. When we were in sight of the Merrey train station, where the Germans were patrolling, I turned around and looked him in the eye.

"You're Jewish, aren't you?"

"No, I threw the star away."

"Be careful at any rate!"

I examined his papers again and felt reassured: the ticket, the pass, everything was in order.

We got on the train and it tickled me to see how easily the Germans had let themselves be fooled. The kid was Jewish, and it was as plain as the nose on your face: the black frizzy hair, the hooked nose, the luminous look in his eyes, that mysterious beauty that characterizes the ancient peoples.

It made me laugh and I said to myself, "So that's the way these Jerries are! I wonder how they would have reacted if there were a Star of David sewn on the Führer's jacket?"

We went through about ten controls before arriving in Paris, and no one suspected that I was dragging around a dirty little Jew destined for the sealed cattle cars and the gas chambers. He had nothing but those papers and a rucksack, which probably contained his tattered clothing. He owned nothing other than that: no biscuits or bonbons, not even a piece of bread nor any money. I had to cut my *frichti* in two so I wouldn't have to watch him die of hunger. At the Gare de l'Est, I opened my coin purse to leave him a little money.

"Here we are in Paris, I suppose you have somewhere to go?"

"You know where you're supposed to take me."

"I do?"

"To the mosque!"

"To the mosque?"

He didn't answer, and I knew there was no use in insisting. We got to the mosque, and I went over to the side entrance and rang the doorbell. Saleh appeared in his djellaba, his teeth rotted from sweets and tobacco.

"Ah, the pretty girl from the Vosges! Have you brought us some onions?"

"No, I've brought you this."

And frowning irritatedly, I motioned toward the child, who suddenly seemed frightened, almost on the verge of tears, he who'd been so sure of himself in the face of the railway employees and the Jerries.

"But I'm not expecting anyone—it's got to be a mistake; that's all it could possibly be," he said, attempting to close the door.

But the boy thrust out his leg to stop him. He'd affected that move so forcefully, it stupefied the Arab and he unintentionally let go of the door.

"Let me come in, Mister, I'm begging you."

The boy still had his leg stuck in the opening, and hot tears were streaming down his cheeks.

"It's a mistake. I'm not expecting anyone. Go on, beat it!"

At that point, the little Jewish boy gained control of his sobs and, with all his might, barked into the Arab's face, "Make haste slowly!"

"All right, all right," said Saleh, having second thoughts and flashing his abominable smile. "Come in, child. And you, get going! You've got no onions? Then get out of here!"

"Make haste slowly!" I didn't understand what that meant until late that night as I was tossing and turning in my bed, literally freezing to death, feeling oppressed by the profound silence in which a nun's dormitory is plunged on a Sunday night. But it was neither the cold nor the anxiety hovering over the austere convent dedicated exclusively to Christ, to prayer, and to sorrow that kept me awake. The little Jewish boy's words ran through my mind over and over. I had heard those words before, a long time ago. They had been embedded deep in my ear so they would never come out again. I had to search through my childhood memories to unravel the puzzle, and when the answer finally came to me, I was able to go to sleep, feeling reassured that I understood a little more about life.

The phrase was from Boileau, I've forgotten the title of the book, but I can still see Mister Le Rognon, the schoolmaster, caressing its thick black cover with red edging. I know it was a book written by Boileau, one of the brightest minds of his time, Mister Le Rognon's mentor. "Make haste slowly!" We'd run into those words everywhere, on the first page of our notebooks, in a corner of the blackboard, in our lectures. The little Jewish boy had come out with them as if he'd been in my class, as if Mister Le Rognon had purposely explained to him what they meant. And then Saleh had calmed down, smiled at him, and the doors to the mosque closed after the boy to protect him from the scourges of the outside world. I was unaware that simple words could have the magical powers of an open sesame. I didn't know that the world often boiled down to obstacles and passwords. It was disastrous, Mister. Mere survival was an act of resistance in itself. Saving your own skin meant saving that of the others as well, all the others.

But that's something one doesn't understand right off the bat. You've got to wait for the end of the nightmare, for everything to stop: the famine and the fear, the military parades, the clattering of trains, the rain of bombs. And only when the vales have begun to take back on their colors, do you realize what you've just narrowly escaped, and how much a word, an insignificant gesture, can contribute to saving a life. Even I participated in the Resistance without being aware of it, without even wanting to, Mister.

After the onions and the episode with the little Jewish boy, I understood why—on certain nights—I heard whispering in the parlor. Understood why I thought I recognized certain voices: that of my father, of your uncle, the mayor, that of Mister Le Rognon, and even that of the Colonel. And why I so often found strangers eating in Mâmiche's kitchen before they disappeared altogether. And the rumors that went around about how sometimes strange shadows would come darting out of the nearby forest (so nearby it touched the Colonel's vegetable garden) and dive into the château! And those moans and coughs coming from the upper floors that my cousins, Nonon Totor's daughters, thought they heard when they went to the château for their piano lessons!

It's all becoming clear now, because the honest folks have spoken out and everything has been written down in books. But at the time, we were in a fog, the trees looked like scarecrows, and human beings did incomprehensible things.

For example, the stranger I ran into one day on his hands and knees, lost in the tall grass on the banks of the Mouzon. I'd gone there to pick tarragon for Mâmiche, and I saw him trying to imitate a dog.

"Which way is Bar-le-Duc?"

"Bar-le-Duc? I've never set foot there!"

"Oh, good God, I did have to run into a little ninny like you. You wouldn't happen to have civilian clothes, would you?"

"Civilian clothes!"

He didn't answer, just kept moving toward the river shimmering a short distance from where we stood. Without taking off his uniform, he dove in and swam with large strokes, then got out of the water, crossed the distance that separated the riverbank from the forest at top speed, and disappeared under the trees.

When I turned back along the road to Romaincourt a few minutes later, I found myself face-to-face with a German soldier who greeted me in perfect French.

"I've lost my prisoner, Miss, you haven't seen him, have you?"

"Of course I have!"

I pointed southward, knowing full well the fugitive had gone north.

"You see over there, after the tall grass and the little island of ferns, over by the abandoned farm, that's where I saw him, sir."

The soldier gave a slight bow and pressed on. In my own way, I had just saved the nation.

What was the connection between Addi, Yolande, Arbuger, the other members of their group, and the Paris mosque? Actually, no one will ever know. When it comes to that question, like everything that has to do with that period, we've only got hearsay and the half-truths that can be found in the books to go by.

Remember that the first mission of the Resistance was to sneak everyone who felt they were in danger into Switzerland and from there, into the free zone. That included lost Tirailleurs, escaped war prisoners, English aviators, Jews, Alsatians who had decided to flee Germanization. And today we know that the Paris mosque was a stronghold of the Resistance and sheltered a great number of Jews. And I know that at least one Jew—mine—left from Romaincourt to make his way to rue Georges-Desplas. There were certainly others, as perhaps there were other times Addi Bâ visited his friends Saleh and Abdallah back in the days when leaving the gray zone was an epic achievement. If not, how to explain that magical Christmas when, after one of his long habitual eclipses, he reappeared offering me chocolate and bringing oranges for my cousins Mathilde and Beatrice—Uncle Hector or Nonon Totor's daughters—to put in their clogs.

There are obscure parts of his life that nothing will ever bring to light now. For example, there's the strange business about Chaumont that would crop up absurdly and unexpectedly in his conversations, sometimes making you doubt his mental health, he who was ordinarily so calm, so reasonable, so sure of himself.

"How far are we from Chaumont?"

He must have put that question to every Vosgian the good Lord set down upon his path, and not one of them fully understood what it meant. It wasn't until after the war, after Colonel Melun, Celestin, and the Pinéguette girl had already been horsing around for quite some time and were on the verge of digging you up over there in Guinea, that we found out a little more about it.

According to Melun, in Harréville-les-Chanteurs, the prisoners of the Twelfth Regiment of Senegalese Tirailleurs had been separated into two groups: one had been assigned to the Rebeval barracks in Neufchâteau and the other to the Frontstalag in Chaumont.

In Neufchâteau Addi had been incarcerated with Fodé, Moriba, Zana, and Diougal, whom I've already told you about. That meant that the others, Tchivellé from the Congo, Moussavou from Gabon, and especially Va Messié from the Ivory Coast (whom everyone considered to be his best friend) were in Chaumont.

Fodé and Moriba had been killed, and Zana and Diougal had disappeared, he knew that. He also knew it was far better to be on the outside, dead or alive, than rotting in a German prison. As reckless and headstrong as I knew him to be, it's quite possible he decided it was his duty to get them out of there: you know, his honor as a friend and soldier and all that malarkey.

We now know that he made a quick stopover in Chaumont on his way to Paris and was seen prowling about the German barracks and asking peculiar questions at the buffet in the train station.

Something else is also intriguing. In Camp Deliverance, he had a shack built off to one side and, gathering a dozen or so recruits around him—including Bertrand and Armand Demange—gave talks that strongly resembled a call to arms.

"Stay alert! I might need you any minute!"

Why had he tried so hard to enter into contact with the Debernardi Resistance network that operated out of Chaumont? Yolande, the most well-informed woman in the Vosges, suspected something. Speaking of which, Etienne remembers a vehement argument (undoubtedly the only one) between the "mama" and the "son" that took place one evening in the small schoolteacher's apartment.

"It's just madness, a childish whim! Do you realize you'll be botching up two years of our work and putting the lives of hundreds of people in danger?"

"I have to get them out of there, Mama! It wasn't a promise—it was an oath!"

"An irresponsible oath, made by a man whose acts are based on emotions, on impulse! Don't force me to doubt in you, Addi Bâ!"

"It can be done. I've calculated all the risks."

"Sending kids out to get killed in a desperate act, is that what you call calculating risks? The Frontstalag in Chaumont is impenetrable and you know it. The Reich decided to ruthlessly exterminate all Gaullists and escaped prisoners, and since then every measure has been taken to accomplish that. No, it will simply be a disaster: it'll get your friends machine-gunned, the people of Chaumont taken hostage, our network decapitated—is that what you want?"

"That's not what happened when we escaped from Neufchâteau."

"Neufchâteau was three years ago. The world has changed a lot since then!"

"You have to understand, Mama!"

"Enough talk, Addi! People have been dragged in front of the disciplinary committee for less than this."

He stepped silently toward her, took her in his arms and they stood there for a long time hugging each other closely, eyes closed, short of breath.

Then he pulled away, glancing at his watch.

"I have to go, Mama. Have a nice evening!"

Addi kept the shack he'd had made over to one side of the camp and did not change his mind, despite the stormy meeting with his "mama." *It's just as well,* he thought to himself, *Chaumont isn't everything; I'll need a* Groupe de Choc *in the coming weeks according to what I hear on Radio Londres.*

— § —

Camp Deliverance was operational and had attracted neither the treacherous tongues of collaborators nor the steely-eyed attention of the Jerries. Addi scoured the neighboring farms to find food and above all to dissuade parents from sending their children to the STO.

Alex and Simon roamed the train stations and the nearby forests, recuperating fugitives and directing them toward the Boène farm.

The Houillons would hide them in the barn until your uncle came to guide them up to the Partisans' Oak. By the end of May 1943, there were as many as five hundred recruits.

The atmosphere was fairly good, despite petty thefts (mostly shoes and cigarettes) and games of ninepins that often ended in brawls. There were no serious accidents or epidemics, and the food supplied was often quite better than what ordinary families could get. Yolande Valdenaire, who knew all the shopkeepers in Petit-Bourg and Saint-André-les-Vosges, brought rice, pasta, cigarettes, and candles. Addi, who'd been adopted by our people, obtained whatever he asked for from the farmers: cheese, milk, eggs, radishes, and cabbage. As for Huguette, she furnished corn flour and bread every week, sometimes even beer.

At reveille they would do exercises, clean the rifles, disassemble and reassemble them, then disassemble them again. For a change of pace, he'd let them play cards, sing bawdy songs, and dance like the Zulus even if it didn't particularly please him. "Oh, if they get a kick out of it," he'd tell himself, "as long as they stand at attention when they see me coming!"

And soon they began yawning, asking the same questions as yesterday and the next day, without really expecting an answer.

"What are we waiting for? Why don't we start fighting?"

"How long are we going to hang around like this?"

"What in the hell are they doing over there in London?"

They weren't the only ones asking questions. Their commander was wondering the very same things. Exasperated, Addi would abruptly put those questions to Yolande or Arbuger, who would again reproach his childish impatience; it was one of the few faults one could find in him.

"London makes the decisions—we're awaiting orders from London!"

"But Mama, they could at least start parachuting weapons in!"

"They'll do that when they think the time has come."

"If they could only send us some explosives! Our carbines will be useless against their tanks. It's explosives that we need."

"Acts of sabotage have been planned and will soon be carried out. Resistance is a concert, son, not cacophony, where everyone trumpets in his own corner."

"Those kids of mine are growing restless, Mama."

"Keep them busy—there's already plenty to do. Just having turned them away from the STO is a great blow to the enemy."

"I'm afraid they'll desert."

"To go where? They're all in the Gestapo's files. They've got very little choice now: it's either our camp or that of the Germans."

"Monotony camp or death camp!"

That kind of discussion could last for hours. In addition to his impatience, she criticized him for his military rigidity—that old-fashioned idea he clung to according to which everything boiled down to willpower, clear-sightedness, and discipline. She'd attempted in vain to make him understand that resisting the occupier necessitated patience and psychology.

"Yeah sure, sure, Mama," he'd respond in the tone of voice of a child who accepts his punishment without admitting he's at fault. For him, the Germans had invaded this country by force, and only force could get them out. If half of France was wallowing shamelessly in cheap German bars, the other half wanted nothing more than to fight. The Gaullists should have been parachuting arms in instead of wasting time conversing in the polished parlors of London with old myopic, half-deaf diplomats.

In those days they'd stopped meeting each other in the small apartment over the school. After having spent the night there once to avoid a storm, Yolande had awakened the next morning and caught sight of a stranger crouching behind the elder bush looking in her direction with binoculars. When she was able to, she would go see your uncle at his place, and they would remain closed up in there for a few minutes. Wearing a scarf over her head that reached down under her chin, with her slight figure, her stealthy steps, her ability to melt into the walls, into the fence posts or the trees, she was almost invisible. When she'd go up to Addi's place or come back out, you really had to keep your eyes peeled to persuade yourself it wasn't a mirage.

For a change of pace, they often met in the forest, in gazebos in public squares, on the platforms of railway stations, or, better yet, right out in broad daylight in the washhouses where they pretended to be scrubbing their laundry. They kept others from hearing them, talking in low voices, exchanging stories like everyone else.

One day she knocked on his door and no one answered. Her knocking was energetic enough for me to hear it in the kitchen where I was working. When I came out on the porch, she was still knocking.

"We haven't seen him for two days!" I remarked.

"Heavens! Probably over at that Zenette's."

It had slipped out unintentionally and I didn't understand right away whether she was speaking of a Suzette, a Zanette, or a Zenette.

"Excuse me, ma'am?"

"No nothing, Miss. If he's been gone for two days, that means he'll be back soon, doesn't it?"

Seeing I didn't answer, she stopped knocking and asked, "Is your father in? Or your mother, or..."

"No, they're all in Fouchécourt for the livestock fair."

"Ah, that's really too bad! How old are you, Miss?"

"Twenty!"

"Could I leave this bag with you? You can give it to him when he comes back."

She jumped on her bike but changed her mind when she reached the war memorial, turned around and added in a quite anxious voice, "Young lady, please don't open it, and, above all, don't give it to anyone else."

Then she rode off again without awaiting my response, probably persuaded that I had no choice but to obey her. I dragged the bag up to my room and hid it under the bed, eyeing the zipper without daring to touch it. But once back in the kitchen, my hands began to prickle as if armies of ants were swarming in my veins. I went back to my room and avidly unzipped the bag. There were only papers, reams and reams of papers held together with paper clips, accompanied by photographs bearing the stamp of the gendarmerie or that of the Feldkommandantur. Today it's easy to conclude they were false identity cards, false passes, false ration cards, false train tickets. But I was only twenty, only just beginning to get a grasp on a world that seemed to get a kick out of slipping just out of my reach.

Once again, I'd put my finger on part of the mystery unfolding around me; that mystery only became completely clear when you arrived here two days ago. Now we have that plaque over there gleaming in the sunlight—it's as precious to us as a diamond found on a street corner; and here you are sitting on this porch and listening to me right in the spot he used to sit so often as well. I have the feeling the story is beginning all over again, since you've got the same name, the same size, the same eyes, the same nose. Since—just as he did—you have the same sparkling smile, those grave deliberate gestures, that tranquil spirit, that tremendous gift of charm, of persuasion that is peculiar to people from your land. The main difference is your starched boubou, that cap embroidered in green and blue, purple and yellow, whereas he most often wore his Tirailleur uniform. The difference is the way you pray—out loud, for everyone to see and hear, whereas he prayed in his room or else over by the grocery store behind the water tank. I look at you and see that you are new, exotic, and distant. You fit in as well with Romaincourt as an acre of palm trees on the snow of Mont Blanc, and I tell myself that Celestin and Colonel Melun—especially the Colonel—and even that Pinéguette were right to do what they did. Without them, you wouldn't be here, Mister. And yet you had to be here in order to come full circle, to make it possible for this story to take on its true meaning, take up its allotted space, so that I—in telling it to you—might truly hear it myself. And yet I almost never even saw you. To begin with, one had to be aware of your existence.

Between their very first contacts with Africa and your presence here, many years went by. Years during which she would have completely brainwashed us, just like they used to do in Cambodia or in China.

They'd split up the tasks, of course, just as anyone who knows how to reach their end would do. Her job was raising people's consciousness, as she used to put it. Leaflets, journalists, demonstrations, meetings. He took care of the grassroots work—archives, ministerial corridors—with the patience of a detective, the rationality of a scholar.

The ministries were never in agreement. Foreign Affairs demanded this paper, the Ministry of Defense that paper, and at the Ministry for Veterans Affairs, they said neither was valid. And when, blushing embarrassedly, the civil servants were forced to take off their glasses and admit that he'd been shamefully overlooked by the Liberation because he was black, when—sixty years after the fact—it was established that the medal was rightfully his, the hardest part began: determining where exactly he came from, getting into contact with his family, and attempting to have his brother, his nephew, a cousin come to take part in the ceremony.

We knew he was born in Guinea, we knew he'd grown up in Langeais. We thought he was from Conakry since that's what his papers claimed, before we realized that civil registries were still in an embryonic state over there and showed all children in the colony to be born in Conakry. Some papers indicated he'd come into the world in 1915, others in 1916 or 1917, depending upon the office Colonel Melun was addressing. The impreciseness of this information was further complicated by another quite significant problem: the situation your country was in at the time. There was already a dictatorship in place, something along the lines of the Soviet Union; a tropical gulag that did not have a Berlin Wall, but one of bamboo that was nevertheless so thick nothing could get in or out except herds of buffalo and swarms of mosquitoes. But that Pinéguette was quite crafty: she thought of Va Messié, your uncle's friend from the Ivory Coast. The Ivory Coast was more accessible than

Guinea. There was still a small chance it might work if Va Messié happened to be alive.

Recalling that a friend she'd encountered at the Sorbonne had married over there, she hurried to write her and received a response immediately. I remember that letter very well, its blue-and-white envelope with red stripes and its large two-inch stamps picturing zebras on the plains in commemoration of who knows what anniversary of the Raoul Follereau Foundation. Pinéguette supplied me with stamps for my collection. She wrote to the entire world, received letters from the entire world: American feminists, Basque nationalists, Nepalese Maoists, anti-apartheid militants, Turkish Kurds, Romanian Gypsies, homosexuals in Amsterdam.

That time she'd been lucky. Beatrice (that was her old friend's name) didn't know the man, but her husband, who was of the same tribe, would make inquiries.

Three months later Pinéguette told us she'd succeeded in meeting Va Messié, who was still alive but in such a poor state of health he couldn't recall if your village was called Bomboli or Bombona. She nevertheless did not give up hope. Va Messié's cook had a neighbor from Guinea who might be able to assist them. That is how we learned the name Pelli-Foulayabé, your true home, a hamlet located only a few flaps of the wing from Bomboli. In the meantime, Guinea had taken on a new dictatorship, one that was pro-Western this time, more open to correspondence and visitors. In a more detailed letter, Beatrice provided us with a slew of information. Addi Bâ's sister and two older brothers had all died, leaving behind numerous children. His younger brother was still alive and had four wives, a son and a daughter. *The boy bears the same name as his uncle. He is the only one in the whole family who knows how to read and write: he's a customs officer who is presently doing an internship in Cuba*, she clarified. When you returned from Cuba, two years later, she sent us another letter: *I would like to know how you intend to present the posthumous medal to the family. If someone must go to France, in my opinion it should be the customs officer, but he hasn't any money, will France pay for his ticket?*

Colonel Melun went back to the ministerial offices, while Pinéguette, believing she was at some sort of rally, went from house to house to get us to cough up: "One hundred euros each, you owe him at least that much!"

You see, your being here is a veritable odyssey. Being here to represent him, so that your face might remind us of his, so that his life will carry on in yours. And I say to myself it's a good thing. I look at you, draped in your boubou, straight-necked, sitting cross-legged in that strange fashion that leads us to believe that everyone over there is in constant communication with heavenly spirits... I look at you and think about what he said after Pascal hung himself.

"Human life is so very tenuous, that's why we all fight so hard to save our own."

That plaque hanging over there bathed in God's light is the sign that he's come back home, that this house will never again feel empty. It not only celebrates a hero, not only repairs an injustice: it liberates us from our doubts; it sets our memory straight once and for all. That man wasn't a passing phantom, glimpsed zigzagging between the trees straddling an old bicycle, perpetually garbed in his Tirailleur uniform. He really lived in Romaincourt; he died for Romaincourt. He is part of the memory of this town: the first man to have a street in the village named after him. Rue Addi-Bâ, now there's a name that says more than School Street or Church Street. If Pinéguette were still alive, she'd be delighted to see it, a shiny new plaque exactly where she'd wanted it, right where the path runs between the two houses, the path upon which the Germans hunted him down and the one she grew up on.

She fought all her life to have him recognized as her father, to have the Vosges, France, the entire world, acknowledge how exemplary his brief passage on earth was. She carried that struggle out night and day with every ounce of ferocity she had in her. That Pinéguette made you think of the animals over there where you live, more like a wildcat than a hippopotamus or a lion. The hippopotamus is heavy; the lion too noble, too arrogant, too proud. She had the quick, simple, and efficient ferocity of the wildcat: she wouldn't scratch; she'd bite just to show off. She'd do it because that was the best way of making sure she'd get what she wanted. Once she'd arrived at her ends, she'd forget all the harm she'd done, as well as all the blows she must have taken too. There was nothing African about her, but she did have a tropical temperament: biblical hurricanes interspersed with peaceful sunny spells.

Now she is definitively at peace in the bosom of Jesus or else petrified in the molten arms of Satan. The man she believed to be her father, who sang her African lullabies and lavished upon her the only caresses of her entire childhood, has now been drawn out of obscurity thanks to her. Perhaps God has absolved her of the many sins she committed, though it is not His nature to absolve demons. I say that, Mister, because it comes straight from my guts, but I do admit I would have felt a sharp pang in my heart if she'd been here, bubbling over with joy at seeing the plaque that devoured her life, standing in the street that, thanks to her, will bear his name from this day onward.

Colonel Melun met you at the airport since she was gone and couldn't welcome you. He drove you to the ceremony in Epinal. I recognized you immediately, not because I was expecting you, not only because of your boubou, but because of that tiny little straight nose, because of that small trim body, because of that voice, that refreshing, level, and powerful voice that we'd heard many times over, right where we're standing under this very roof. No one, not even the mayor, had time to ask you the questions that were stuck in all of our throats. We had to have a hurried lunch so we wouldn't be late getting to Mount Virgin, where he was executed, but then you disappeared in the ocean of kepis and top hats milling around. Everyone wanted to greet you, get a good close look at you, glorify your uncle and say something nice about you or your country. It was the same at the Partisans' Oak and later here in Romaincourt.

I felt like pulling you aside and saying, "Come with me, those people don't know anything. I'm the one who kept his photographs and his letters, his Koran and his military papers. He used to listen to the radio at my parents' house; he used to embroider over at Mâmiche Léontine's. I served as his messenger in Paris, though I was completely unaware of it. In the end, I finally made up my mind to wash his socks, though he was completely unaware of it. Come with me, it's all so clear in my mind that I sometimes believe I can feel his breath or hear the sound of his footsteps! They'd planned on putting you up in a hotel. A hotel, now that was out of the question, not as long as I'm alive! You are to sleep where he slept, eat where he ate—that's what he would have wanted if he could have shouted it out from the necropolis over in Colmar.

Sixty years is nothing! When he died, your father was a child, I was a sweet young teenager, and you hadn't yet been jotted down on the good Lord's to do list. Sixty years! The calendar can say whatever it pleases. Nothing will keep me from thinking that it all happened this morning, last night at the latest. That's how old age works, Mister: it unearths old memories in order to better lay the present to rest. You arrived here before your uncle, that's what my mind wants to make me believe.

That particular Saint Nicholas' Day, or the day of Saint Bartholomew Pig Feast if you prefer, is brand-new, absolutely intact in a corner of my brain, and when I call it to mind, it's as if it were the present and were happening right now.

I'd had a little bit too much plum brandy that evening, and I knew he didn't like that or our village fetes with the throbbing music and the horrendous smell of pork meat and moonshine. And yet he never missed one. He wove the lasting ties that still bind him to this land at our communions, baptisms, Christmases, and Saint Nicholas' Days. He struck up friendships and inspired confidence in the vast majority of people at those family celebrations. He shut his eyes to the ham, the plum brandy, joked with everyone, and got to his feet when asked to dance a few steps of our traditional *soyotte*.

That evening I'd forced him to dance more than he wanted to because I'd been drinking, because I wanted to keep him busy, prevent him from repeating the words he'd just uttered.

"When you've finished growing up, Germaine, I'll suggest that this young man become your fiancé." Pointing to young Etienne, who was a bit giddier than I was.

Vexed that he should say that in front of everyone, I played upon his most sensitive point: his reputation as a heartbreaker, the secret side of his life. I say secret because everyone looked the other way out of respect for the "Sergeant."

And as I was whirling him around, I answered, "A fiancé? But, my handsome Tirailleur, I should propose one for you if you didn't already have so many." And he made that legendary frown of his and repeated for the umpteenth time the words I would hear only once more, the night just before he was arrested: "I'll straighten you out, Germaine! *Wallâhi*, I'll straighten you out!"

That evening a confused feeling took root in my heart. As I danced with him, I glanced quickly at Etienne to see if he'd make a proper fiancé. I'd always considered him to be an unpolished, ordinary, naïve, grinning teenager who, like all the boys in the Vosges, was an amateur hunter, ninepins player, and mushroom gatherer. For the first time, I was seeing him as a man and, undoubtedly influenced by Addi Bâ's words, I found something mature, something virile, something seductive about him. I was falling in love with him, and perhaps the same thing was happening to him. At your uncle's suggestion, that evening marked the beginning of a long infatuation for him and an all-encompassing passion for me. His mop of blond hair and his eyes that resembled those of Louis Jouvet had made me completely forget Pascal.

In our country, Mister, cousins are traditionally promised in marriage to one another, and I learned from your uncle that the exact same tradition exists in your land. I was pledged to Pascal very early on. My parents were planning to celebrate the engagement as soon as he'd come back from his tour of France. But you already know that unhappy ending.

Oh, don't think I'm in any way bitter about it. Life has taught me how to miss a turn and turn the page. One can't build a future if one doesn't take the trouble to close the door on the ghosts of the past. I don't hold a grudge against Asmodée for having taken my Pascal away, Mister. I hold a grudge against her for having destroyed him. I hold a grudge against her for having stuck the handsome name of Tergoresse on to her bastards.

But it's not easy to turn the page. As hard as you might try, you'll always find a bit of grief to gnaw on. I was still gnawing on what was left of mine when your uncle arrived. Can you imagine, the first black man in the village, so impressive in spite of his small stature, smiling, well-kempt, distinguished. Someone who, at a time when his race was considered to be the most brutish of all humanity, succeeded in gaining the respect of an entire French township.

In secret, I started transferring the love I had harbored for Pascal to him. I dreamt that the war was over. I pictured him in a colonel's uniform coming and kneeling before my father to ask for my hand. All of Romaincourt in white dresses and velvet suits following me down to the boat, skipping to the rhythm of a magnificent nuptial fanfare, the children holding calico banners and the adults garlands of flowers. Over there, of course, he would have been king, and I queen. And we would have had a palace on the banks of a large river winding through the baobabs, through herds of buffalo and zebra. It was a secret love, a terrifying and impossible love. I forced myself to think of it as little as possible. In his presence, I pretended to be a spoiled little brat, or flippantly indifferent, for fear he would suspect something. I almost kissed him the night he talked to me about young Etienne, but I managed to control myself.

The next day, however, it was Etienne's face that lingered in my mind. Point to a camel and tell me, "That's what love is!" My heart will believe you without hesitation. When I awoke, I jumped on my bike and followed the path to Petit-Bourg. I rode past his house, where I knew he'd be in the courtyard splitting wood.

"Good day, Etienne!"

"Look, here's Germaine! You never come by this way—what's gotten into you?"

"My parents sent me over to Saint-André-les-Vosges to trade some cheese for ham."

"Ah, so you'd like for me to come along with you? My parents are at the hospital in Nancy!"

"Then your father's lungs aren't any better?"

"No!" he said, hanging his head as if to hide his shame. "So I'll come along with you."

"Not at all!" And I immediately regretted having said that.

"Aha! You're afraid, are you? A boy and a girl, out riding bikes together in the middle of the countryside..."

"I just don't want you to come with me, that's all!"

"And what if we met tomorrow on Sapinière ridge? What do you think about what the Sergeant said?"

"I don't think anything about what the Sergeant said," I shouted as I rounded the curve.

After having done the dishes and the laundry for Mâmiche, who was stuck in bed with a nasty migraine, I walked across the garden and took a few steps toward the ridge. I wasn't going for the meeting, I wasn't going to see him. For that matter, he hadn't mentioned any particular time. I was going because I often roamed around up there to smell the pines and see the squirrels running about.

"Ah! There she is!" shouted a voice behind me as I bent over to pick a flower.

"I didn't come out here to see you, Etienne!"

"I didn't say anything! I know of a lovely stream on the other side of the hill, in the direction of Méricourt. I could catch some nice silver catfish for you over there."

"Only if you promise not to talk to me about what the Tirailleur said."

There never were any silver catfish because we never got to that stream. As soon as the vegetation began to get dense around us, he laid his hand on my shoulder. And when he saw that I didn't object, he moved it up into my hair and stuck his lips on mine and tilted me over onto the leaves. I was eighteen years old, and it was the first time I'd kissed a boy.

It lasted till the end of the war, till he left for Paris. We would meet secretly in the woods or on the country paths to neck and dream about our future. He never talked about himself, only from time to time he'd mention the nightmare he was living through in the thatched cottage in Petit-Bourg.

What I'm going to tell you now is not very nice, but one day I saw the two of them, Yolande and your uncle, go up to his room. It was the first time that had ever happened. They stayed up there a long time, whereas Yolande Valdenaire's visits usually never lasted longer than a few minutes.

Intrigued, I went up and put my ear to the door. This is what I heard, "I've fixed up a bed for myself in the storeroom."

"Don't you love him anymore, Mama?"

"I don't know, I'm not sure anymore. I'm afraid."

"Afraid of not loving him?"

"Love's not enough, Son. I need to feel admiration."

"Does he know you're seeing me?"

"He suspects so. At first he'd blow up at me. Now there's just utter silence between us, as with all couples when there's nothing much left."

"What about Etienne?"

"He keeps quiet and just endures it like a well-mannered child."

"It's all my fault, isn't it?"

"You just happened to have been in the wrong place at the wrong time."

"This is war, Mama!"

"You blame the war on everything. Is it due to the war that you fall in love with every woman in the Vosges? Your nightlife is starting to make people talk. Do you really need all these women?"

"I don't drink or smoke, Mama. I need some distraction, Mama. You're not jealous, are you?"

"A little."

"What's happening to us, Mama?"

"I don't know. Let's wait for the war to come to an end; things will be clearer then."

"Yes, the words will come easier afterward."

"Tell me about this Zenette girl!"

He started laughing.

"I don't much like that laugh, Addi. It's the way you laugh whenever a question makes you uncomfortable."

That's exactly when I sneezed, they opened the door, and I turned as red as a beet and babbled out a thousand apologies.

After the war, that part of the story never grew any clearer in my poor old head. One was the "mother," the other the "son." Their two yearning bodies desired each other without ever, ever daring to touch one another. Everyone had guessed as much, but no one in the Vosges allowed themselves to mention it, either in the days of the Resistance or afterward.

I admire those two's spirit of sacrifice, Mister. I admire their painful and passionate, yet chaste relationship even more. They were as capable of withstanding the assaults of love as they were those of the war, as capable of living clandestinely as they were of facing death.

For me, your uncle represented the two faces of Janus. When there was a man in my life, he was a father figure, but when there wasn't, he took on the traits of Romeo. From the Saint Bartholomew Pig Feast up until the execution squad, he was the father figure. Now that he's dead and the fiancé he picked out for me has left, he will forever incarnate the love I was never able to experience.

And yet young Etienne and I had gotten off to a good start. The first year, his packages and postcards poured in twice a week, then they grew more spaced out and ended up disappearing altogether. I swallowed my pride and wrote him a letter. His answer was quick: *We were so young, my sweet Germaine! You didn't really believe in the Sergeant's joke, did you?*

I locked myself up in my room for a month, ashamed of my bloodshot eyes.

I received the final blow the next Christmas when the town started passing his marriage announcements around. So I began taking out the pictures of your uncle, leafing through the Koran and caressing his Tirailleur uniform.

Years went by and I thought I'd forgotten Etienne when he came back home to inform us he'd just been divorced and he bitterly regretted not having married Germaine.

He knocked at our door, threw himself at my feet, and pleaded with me to forgive him.

"After everything you've put me through?"

I was obliged to say that out of pride. I thought he would understand, that he'd keep trying until I gave in, until the love that was burning within had reduced me to ashes.

"You should have accepted," he simply said when we ran into one another at the shooting concession at the Fouchécourt fair.

And a few months later, that loony girl from Brittany turned up in the Vosges. She said she was an ornithologist with a passion for the wood grouse, an endangered species that she claimed she would save from our nefarious human behavior. The woman went to see Etienne, ostensibly because she'd heard about his hunting talents, but in truth it was to sink her claws into him. However, her conceited airs, her legendary indiscretion, and her deep fondness for whiskey ended up incurring the contempt of everyone around here. And since there wasn't a wood grouse to be found as far out as the Alsatian border, she turned away from grouse in order to devote herself to the sooty albatross of Australia.

Etienne came back to see me the day before the long journey.

"Aw, it was only a youthful crush that leaps back to life every now and again and makes our hearts flutter. Let's just be friends, Germaine!"

I didn't bear a grudge against him. In truth, I'm not even sure that it upset me. Mama and Papa were dead, so was Mâmiche Léontine. I could have drawn the curtains and cried for a year if I'd wanted to, but I didn't. I realized that I just wasn't made for love, and I didn't have many tears left to cry about anything anymore. So Etienne became a friend; it was a consolation after the devastation Pinéguette had caused—a barrier against the monotony of this modern-day Romaincourt where, except for the Rapennes, there's hardly a soul to talk to anymore.

I'm eighty years old, Mister. I live off of my memories now. I only have Sunday mass and the postcards from Australia to look forward to.

I get as worked up about them as the ones he used to send me from Paris, when our love was as fresh as roses.

He's got a good heart, Etienne does, as opposed to that Pinéguette. A trifle scatterbrained, a bit naïve, a little weak in character. I sure would have made him happier than that hussy from Brittany who cut him off from his homeland and took him to the other end of the earth.

Of course, I thought about marrying back then. All young women think about it at that age. It was long afterward that I understood human beings can do without that kind of vanity.

When I returned from Paris, I began helping the priest because the church is right next door and because I didn't have anything else to do. No one had any use for a seamstress within a hundred miles of here. The ration cards had disappeared along with the war, but we still ate just as little and just as poorly as before. The priest was in need of a *bâbette*-servant: he talked with my father, who used to call me into his room whenever he had something important to tell me.

"The priest's servant is an admirable position for a young girl in your situation. Now you aren't going to complain, are you?"

I hadn't the slightest desire to complain. I couldn't have found a better position. A respectable job only a few steps from the house at a time when no salary would be considered too small. I didn't think I would work there all my life, I thought it would simply be a means of passing the time, until someone else popped up to walk me down the aisle. I saw a dozen or so priests appointed before I retired, and no one, except Alphonse Rapenne, Cyprien's cousin, ever came and to ask for my hand. I would have said yes, even to that short-legged Alphonse, who smelled of garlic and moonshine, whose hair was always sticky with sweat. But something I couldn't have foreseen occurred. Papa,—Papa whom I'd always seen smiling, helpful, and level-headed—burst into my room like a tornado.

"I won't have it! I won't have a Rapenne in my home!"

I thought those old family feuds could affect almost anyone except a man as high-principled as my father. Alphonse is the same age as I am. We pass each other at church from time to time, when he's able to walk. We talk about the good old days—meaning your uncle, who finds his way into every conversation and whose photo hangs in the majority of parlors around here. He comes over at times to have some chamomile tea, and we laugh about what used to make us cry, both agreeing that in Romaincourt, less people die of the croup and the war than of the ancestral hatred between the Rapennes and the Tergoresses.

A star comes loose up in heaven when someone dies, he confided to me once when winter was so harsh he grew despondent and homesick. And you know, it's true. The evening of his death, I saw a star break loose from the Big Dipper, go ripping through the sky with the resonance of a blowtorch, and end up being furiously snuffed out as it plunged into the Meuse. And don't go telling me it was a dream. You don't pinch yourself in a dream to make sure it's real.

There's no doubt his father saw that star fall too, from across the sea. I can picture the way it happened very clearly. Sitting under the veranda, fingering his beads, he suddenly felt something vibrate in the sky. So he took his cap and his cane and, without saying anything to the mother, went down through the ferns and the latanias till he reached the slope leading to the river. The old man stood up tall on the bank with that meditative look you all have in your eyes, and he waited for a long, long time before the star came crashing into the water. Then, remembering word for word what the witch doctor had said, he made his way to the sacred termite mound to make an offering.

— § —

The father's prayer skin and the mother's milking gourd, the village at the top of the hill and the river down below, winding through the gorges... He didn't talk about himself but he talked about the village, about the smell of honey and hot taro, the terrifying rush of the herds entering the corrals, the languorous sound of flutes. It didn't bother him to talk about all that, and he would so often that I felt as if I'd lived there myself and had been there when the witch doctor took out his mirror. But you're the one who told me about that. He'd barely mentioned the witch doctor, uttering the word in such an enigmatic fashion, I was under the impression he was trying to pull the wool over our eyes.

"Why should a black man fight for the liberation of France?" I asked him.

"Because of the witch doctor!" he responded.

"What about slavery? What about colonization?"

"The fire that has burned you is the same that will warm you."

"But it's as if you were trying to liberate your jailers. Black men fighting for France and Frenchmen for Germany!"

"There's a name for that, Germaine: human absurdity."

"What does the witch doctor have to do with it?"

"Calm down, Germaine! I promise I'll answer your questions someday. But for now I have to fight this war, no matter who the enemy is. No one will ever be able to say that Addi Bâ turned tail."

"Today the enemy is Hitler!"

"The enemy is death, that's the only enemy worth standing up against!"

Now that you've resolved the enigma, his life lies before me like a puzzle that's just been completed. His silence has become edifying and his proverbs much clearer.

You say he was born in the year of the earthquake, which, according to your calculations, corresponds to the year 1916. It seems the village recalls it very well: a comet had been seen, and lightning had hit the corral killing dozens of cattle. And the next morning, down by the river the heavy sound of drums was heard. A few instants later, a rugged young man whose face was covered with scars came to the entrance of the village.

"We are Bambaras! Will you allow us to enter?"

The gate of vines had been opened for him, and the witch doctor walked in followed by his blind wife and his drum players. He walked straight over to your grandfather's hut without asking the way.

"Peuhl, give me an ox, and I will show you my mirror!"

"I've already got one!"

"There is no mirror like mine. Look!"

He put it under your grandfather's nose, and he saw what there was to see.

The next day, the muezzin's son fell from the top of a locust bean tree and died while he was being transported to the dispensary in Bomboli. It was the exact scene that had unfolded in the mirror.

"Peuhl, I know you've just had a baby boy and that's why I've come. The boy is not an ordinary boy. The gods have tattooed his soul: he will be famous. Except..."

"Except?"

"Except, the child does not belong to you. Someone will come to take him away."

"And what is the name of this someone?"

"The gods have not told me his name."

He held out the mirror again, "Here, look!"

"A white man?"

Your grandfather examined the image that appeared in the mirror for a long time. It was a white man like all white men, dark-haired and obese with a cane and a frock coat, a top hat and a thick butterfly mustache. He uttered the name of Allah several times, acknowledging the marvels of the mirror and the unexpected destiny that had been bestowed upon his newborn son.

"You'll recognize him—he will be the only white man you will ever see with your own two eyes."

"And he will sell the boy, is that right?"

"The gods have not foreseen that. Your son must leave here as soon as you have circumcised him. Do not hold him back, it could bring you misfortune."

"Then why didn't the gods have him born white?"

"Because they don't need anyone's permission. That's all I can tell you: this child is not from here. He will live his true life over there, and over there he will lose it. You will take him down to the riverside, and the white man will take him from your hands, and you will never see him again."

"My son!"

"I tell you he is not your son! Here he would be but a rough draft. The gods only begin people's lives. We each create ourselves on this earth. Over there, with the white people in the land of the cold, is where he will be truly born. His life, his true name, and his grave are to be found over there! Now give me my ox, I must return to Ségou!"

The Bambara had walked some thousand kilometers to deliver that news. Ten years later, the chief of the Bomboli township sent a message to the village.

"Soon someone will be coming from Conakry to collect taxes."

The next Wednesday down by the river, shouts of frightened children running out of the water where they'd been swimming rang out, bringing sudden panic upon the small bush village habitually plunged in silence and resignation.

"A white man! It's true, a white man!"

The inhabitants came out of their huts, climbing atop termite mounds and up into trees to get a better look. It was a white man, a real white man: as bizarre and indescribable as they'd always imagined. The women felt like fleeing, and the children like keeping their eyes shut tight. But the man was white. They had to empty out their best huts to house him and his Senegalese Tirailleurs, his servants, and his hammock bearers. They had to take off his shoes, fan him, put up his mosquito net. They had to slaughter an ox, heat water for his bath. It was impossible not to smell him, impossible not to touch him, not to see him! After three days of feeling terrorized and queasy, the people gathered around him to listen to his message. "If you have banknotes, it is preferable; if not, you can give whatever you want: chickens, goats, sheep, oxen, rice, fonio, millet, corn... Do you understand?" The silos and corrals were searched in order to bring him what he wanted. And you told me it was the most uncomfortable night your grandfather ever spent in his life. The secret was oppressing him—he had not told anyone about it. He'd spoken of the matter with the Bambara alone in the privacy of the hut he inherited from his father and where he received his wives each in turn. What could he say to the white man? Just when that question was crossing his mind, a different, more unbearable, more unanswerable question swooped down upon him: how would he be able to explain it to his wife Néné, the child's mother? He spent the night racking his brains, sprawled out on the gravel in the courtyard, dazzled by the moonlight, irritated by the abominable chorus of crickets and toads. But the next day, eyelids swollen from lack of sleep and lips frozen with dread, he remarked that things were in fact going quite well and quite quickly, as if the Bambara's mirror had not forgotten him.

After having had his breakfast, the white man asked for some papaya, a fruit he seemed particularly fond of. All of the boys vied to be the first to go and pick some. The fastest one returned ten minutes later with a calabash filled with nice ripe pink papaya cut up into chunks.

"Thank you, boy! Who does he belong to?"

"To me!" shouted your grandfather proudly.

"What is his name?"

"Addi Bâ!"

"He's a handsome lad for a pickaninny!"

"I'll give him to you!"

At last he could pronounce the words he had rolled around on his tongue for so long without daring to utter them. Before, he wouldn't have had the strength; afterward, no one would have paid any attention.

The white man turned toward his Tirailleurs, who were all cracking up.

"He's giving me his son! Do you hear?"

They were doubled over laughing; no one could answer.

"What shall I do with him?"

"You're asking me what you should do with your son?"

The white man's face suddenly turned grave again, and a hint of discomfort glinted deep in his eye. He mumbled something, glancing down at the floor, looking like a schoolboy surprised at the severity of a punishment. *Wonderful,* thought your grandfather, *he's good and confused now. The mirror has him by the throat, but he can't know that—he only knows white man's things. He knows nothing about the mirror.* He looked him straight in the eye, in exactly the same way sorcerers neutralize their victims. He knew he was the victor and that everything which had been written in the stars would be fulfilled. The Bambara could not have come from so far away to make a false prophecy.

The white man was sweating. He took out his handkerchief and brought it mechanically to his throat, as if he were smothering. Then he looked at his watch and mumbled, in a defeated tone of voice, "Very well, very well..." and, turning toward his

Tirailleurs, "what are you waiting for? Tie my shoes and bring out my trunks!"

The white man swallowed his last chunk of papaya and quickly rinsed his fingers. His Tirailleurs picked him up delicately and placed him in the center of the hammock. The column started off toward the river followed by the village in a joyous throng with the women and children waving their hands and chanting out songs of *adieu*.

The white man crossed the river and stood shaking your grandfather's hand for a long time.

"You've won—he's my son! But I must admit, I still don't know what I'm going to do with him!"

Your grandfather withdrew his hand and turned back before the mirror could change its mind. His wife, whom he'd temporarily succeeded in dispelling from his mind, suddenly appeared, standing like a lioness in front of the fence of vines that encircled the village.

"Ibrahima, you are going to tell me what you've done with my child right this minute!"

In twenty years of marriage, it was the first time she'd ever called her husband by his first name. It was so undignified, so unprecedented that he felt a trickle of sweat run down the back of his neck.

"He's gone off with the white man. Don't try to tell me you didn't see that. He's going to sell him, isn't he?"

"Who told you that, you silly little fool? He's just going to visit Conakry. He'll be back for Tabaski."

"Ibrahima, that's not what my innermost fibers are telling me."

"We'll talk about it tomorrow, Néné. Go and make me some kinkéliba—can't you see I've got a migraine?"

"Why did you do this?"

"To save us from the end of the world."

He disappeared into his hut and plunged himself into the most drawn-out prayers of his lifetime. He awoke the next day with a pain sharper than that of a tumor. He hurried to wake his wife. Though she could not help him find a solution, she alone could share in his grief.

"Do you know I didn't even think to ask his name?"

"Ibrahima, who told you that white men have names?"

You had to come here in order for the enigma of the witch doctor to be resolved. So that is how Addi Bâ was adopted by Maurice Maréchal, a man who originally came from Langeais in the Touraine region and who served as a tax collector in Conakry. Three years after that, when Mr. Maréchal retired, the two of them took a boat for France. Your uncle was thirteen years old. The photographs from Langeais show a boy who was well-treated, judging by his brand-new bicycle, his patent leather shoes, and his gabardine suit. Over there, he's remembered as an obliging youngster who would cut wood for old ladies and do odd jobs for Dr. Pellet, the mayor of the town.

Your uncle's arrival in Romaincourt depended on a Bambara walking from Ségou to Fouta Djallon and on the Valdenaires going out picking mushrooms...

What we call "destiny" is a rather highfalutin word. In truth it's simply a series of little fluke happenings nestled one into the other. An apple falls in Ardèche and there's a tsunami in Peru! How much do we understand about the interplay of blood and tears our lives happen to unfold in?

In your opinion, if those courageous farmers hadn't revolted, if the German tanks hadn't been stationed around the fountain, if your uncle hadn't ventured outside to quench his excruciating thirst, if... would he have encountered Brigadier Thouvenet? Of course not, and without Brigadier Thouvenet, without Etienne and his love of mushrooms, without you having come here, this story wouldn't exist. The brigadier's role is subtle and secondary, therefore essential in the unraveling of the story. You'll recall their unfortunate encounter in a prison cell, the game of chance pitting life against death that the two of them had played at the railway crossing.

I only saw that Thouvenet man once or twice in my life. The first time, the mayor had just given your uncle his papers and civvies. The brigadier was making his rounds when he noticed him sitting, as he often did, on the steps of the church. He jumped into his van along with a squad of subordinates.

"*Môn!* Lord! What's that nigger doing there?"

"Why it's..."

The gendarme winked to let him know he should keep quiet and walked toward him with his hand on the holster of his revolver.

"Have you got any papers? I'm talking to you, nigger!"

Your uncle rummaged around in his pockets while the gendarme put on his glasses.

"Uh-huh, a farmhand! It could be a sham, eh? To operate your little contraband operation, or worse yet! I'll have to verify this—show me where you live!"

A crowd gathered. The population of Romaincourt decided something very grave was happening. Before the war they hadn't the slightest inkling that brigades of gendarmes existed. A hundred or so pairs of eyes followed your uncle, escorted by the edgy gendarmes. They had him walk up the main street, turn right, walk past the porch, and push open that door on the other side of the sidewalk, which at the time was just a single door. When he passed over the threshold, the brigadier turned sternly to his colleagues and said, "Wait here and don't come in unless I give the order to do so!"

They remained closed up in there for over a quarter of an hour. People found it quite long for a simple identity check, but they weren't terribly put out about it.

The second time was right in this parlor. One night when there was such a heavy snowstorm that, after having listened to the radio, your uncle stayed over chatting with Papa waiting for it to die down a little. We heard a vehicle come to a stop, then there was a faint knock at the door. The gendarme came bursting into the alcove exhaling plumes of steam. He sat down for just a few seconds. However, I noticed that he took the time to lean quickly toward your uncle's ear and that my presence seemed to displease him. That wasn't enough to make me suspect he was a member of the Resistance. Later I pretended to slip away into the kitchen but hid in the hallway, keeping my ears open, and what I heard ended up persuading me that the era we were living in was completely haywire.

"That convoy of yours didn't reach Switzerland last week, Addi! It fell straight into the hands of the Gestapo. There was an old lady amongst them who had a cough. How many times do I have to tell you? Only the able-bodied! I don't want people who limp or cough. Be careful, if someone must be nabbed, it won't be me. Understand?"

Wartime is so strange! Black men fighting in the Resistance, Frenchmen betraying their own country, Germans admiring Berlioz, Baudelaire, and Beaujolais, gendarmes siding with outlaws. Who was the victim, who the villain? It wasn't easy for the child I was to distinguish Good from Evil, the lamb from the wolf. My mind was total chaos, filled with fog and confusion! There were no distinct lines between countries or between the way people behaved either.

Not all Germans were bastards, meaning that most of them were especially so: the SS or *essesses* as they were called here. The Feldkommandantur did its job without being overly zealous—that helped to save a few human lives. With the Gestapo, you had the choice between the gallows and the gas chamber, at the Feldkommandantur, they gave you a slim third chance.

On the French side, it was the police who were overly zealous. The gendarmerie closed its eyes to contraband and secret meetings as much as it could and sometimes even helped people escape to Switzerland.

As for the Resistance—well, to be truthful, it was more like a remote boarding school out in the middle of the woods, a roughly hewn, weather-beaten boys' camp. They played cards or Zulus or checkers; they took gibes at the gossipmongers and the clergy. Their commander contented himself with being an observer. He was only intransigent about three things. As I've already told you, they were to stand at attention as soon as he arrived, most importantly, they were never to leave camp without his permission, and they were never to receive strangers in the camp except those that he brought in.

The boys respected those rules to a T, even that tall Armand lad, who wasn't such a bad sort after all.

That's the way things went along for four months. Addi would spend the day with the men, taking part in their games, teaching them how to handle the carbines and the machine guns. By night, he took up his mysterious comings and goings, making the rounds to the flour mills and the farms, meeting up with Simon, Alex, or Aunt Armelle in the most peculiar places.

Their conversations grew more bitter as the waiting drew out. The boys couldn't stand sitting around idly any longer, and he understood how they felt.

"If this keeps up, I'm going to take action, Simon," Addi Bâ threatened.

Simon sighed wearily. That was always his response when he was at a loss for new arguments. Deep down, he too felt the same way, was burning with the same impatience but felt helpless. The hierarchy had ordered him to act solely under instructions, to obey orders, to strictly obey orders. He knew from his frequent conversations with Gauthier that actions were under way, preparations were progressing, but all of that took time. They had to proceed so very meticulously! One mistake, just one simple oversight would mean complete disaster.

"The Germans are like Bengal tigers, Addi: either you kill them or you get killed. Wounded, they're much more dangerous."

"Yeah sure, let's just hang around doing nothing, waiting for the landings that will never happen. Sometimes I feel like I'm wasting my time, Simon, and that's something that really irks me."

"Paratroopers will be dropped soon, and we'll be able to start in."

"We could already start in. Acts of sabotage don't require heavy material. Just a small contraption is enough to get a dig at the enemy."

"There's one word you'll never be able to get through your head: 'coordination.' What good will it do for you to run around on your own up at Camp Deliverance while the men in Lozère and the Haute-Seine aren't even aware of our existence? You're a soldier after all, Addi!"

They separated without saying good-bye, and the encounter he had with Yolande the next day was not any pleasanter.

"We'll wait for orders from London. It's impossible to do otherwise! In the meantime, have them play hopscotch if you like, and you—try and rein in your libido!"

"We're not asking for much, just a few missions to carry out. We need to show those Germans they can't always be on the winning side, don't we?"

"London will let us know what we are to do and when!"

"Mama..."

"Don't answer back, Son. Go and get some sleep. It's warm out tonight; there'll be patrols all over the place."

He spent a very depressing week. Then one night, Marcel Arbuger—alias Simon—knocked at his door using the code they'd agreed upon. He jumped out of bed with his heart nearly leaping out of his chest, telling himself that if Simon was knocking at the door at this hour, something very important must have happened. But when he opened the door, he was greeted with a wide smile. A smile that—rather than being reassuring—made him even more nervous. Perhaps Marcel was taunting him? The man had come expressly to test his nerves, knowing how much this interminable wait had put him on edge. He motioned him to come in and say nothing. They would talk once they were up in his room. But he didn't have time to start up the stairs because Simon grabbed him by the shoulders.

"I've got something for you at last!"

Addi did not react, thinking it was a joke.

"Just listen. First of all, a group of deserted German officers need to get to Switzerland. These are big fish, a mine of information. London needs them to make it over there alive and without losing a single document."

Seeing a gleam of interest beginning to kindle in Addi's eyes, Simon went on with heightened enthusiasm.

"Are you familiar with Fouchécourt?... No? That's really too bad. Around the outskirts of that charming village, the Germans have stocked their largest reserve of war booty: machine guns abandoned by the French army. Guillaume thinks it's time to get hold of them to prepare for the landings. And he's just received London's go-ahead. And just guess who the lucky little man in charge of organizing the operation is going to be?"

Addi slapped him on the shoulder and shook his hand vigorously in response.

"It will be your chance to put your protégés to the test. But that's not all: a train loaded with wood and SS officers on furlough is leaving for Germany next week. That train will be derailed—take care of that on your own!"

"Is that an idea from London?"

"No, from Gauthier."

After the war, I was able to check my information. A group of terrorists attacked an ammunitions depot in Fouchécourt. The result being three dead and many wounded. The other bit of news that made a lot of noise at the time was the unexplained burning of a railway car headed for Germany at the train station in Merrey. The upshot of that: five SS officers killed and the whole load of wood destroyed.

One evening around midnight near the end of June, an unusual sound startled the whole camp. After having shared a *frichti* with his boys and dispensed the last recommendations for the day, Addi Bâ was preparing to make the rounds and collect supplies or, who knows, perhaps go out for one of his amorous encounters.

"I hear footsteps!" said Bertrand worriedly.

"Yes, so do I," added someone else. "It sounds like they're coming closer."

"Let me go out and see what it is, Sergeant!" said Armand.

"Not alone! Bertrand, pick three of your boys to go with him, and don't forget your arms of all things! Now, shhh! Not another word!"

It could have been wild boars, roe deer, poachers, escapees, who knows, Germans readying to attack. As a precaution, Addi Bâ had the campfire extinguished, posted sentinels, and told his boys to prepare for combat. Then the distant and panic-stricken voice of Armand broke the silence.

"Sergeant, come quick—we've got them!"

Addi Bâ rushed out with a dozen boys or so, ordering the others to guard their positions. They braved the forest with the glow of their flashlights, guided by Armand's voice, which they could hear every two or three minutes. They found them less than five hundred meters from there: twelve blond officers in German uniforms, hands in the air, in the custody of Armand

and his companions. It was a fine catch. They dragged them up to the camp, where they were tied up prior to interrogation.

"Does anyone speak German?"

"I do a little bit, Sir. My mother is Alsatian you know!"

"Very well, Armand, interrogate the good men, so we can find out what they had in store for us."

"I'd like to Sir, except..."

"What, Armand?"

"Their German is as incomprehensible as their French."

Addi Bâ cursed and turned nervously toward the prisoners.

"Czechs, Romanians, Croatians?"

"Russians!" they answered in almost perfect unison.

There followed an hour of cacophonic conversation, a surrealistic mélange of Bavarian and French, of Lorraine patois and Alsatian. They came to the understanding that these young men, who had been conscripted into the army commanded by Vlasov (the Russian general who had joined forces with Hitler), had decided to desert and join the French Resistance.

Some of the boys rejoiced loudly; others, like Armand, were dubious.

"How can we be sure they're deserters, Sir? They could just as well be spies. I demand they be executed on the spot!"

"That would be idiotic! Let them talk first!"

"I agree with you, Bertrand, and this is what I've decided: they'll tell us everything from now until sunrise, if not, we will kill one of them every hour. To begin with, how did they learn of our existence?"

He drew out his revolver and aimed at the head of the man who seemed the meekest, asking Armand to translate as well as he could.

"All right, let's begin with you! Who told you about this camp?"

"The Germans!"

"Which Germans?"

"The ones who left us in the forest."

"You see, Sir, they aren't alone—they have accomplices in the forest. What are we waiting for? Let's shoot them!"

"Calm down, Armand. Ask these jerks to lead us to the two Germans."

"Yes, where are they hiding? And why didn't they come with you?"

"Because they're Germans, and you would surely have executed them. They thought we would have a little bit more of a chance. At any rate, now we're all done for. If we go back to the camp, we'll be shot, likewise if we stay here. But we've got a better chance over on this side."

"Very well, you and two of your friends are going to lead us to these Germans. Armand, come with us, and you, Bertrand, stay here to hold down the camp. If the slightest alert is given, kill all of these Russian dogs!"

There were two of them all right, Germans from head to toe, holed up in a cave, but Germans nonetheless, meaning self-confident and stiff in their handsome non-commissioned officers' uniforms. They raised their hands spontaneously and allowed themselves to be led to the camp with astonishing docility. Once there, they repeated what the Russians had already said: they had deserted in order to join the French Resistance, but, since they were German and not Russians, Croatians, or Slovenians, they thought they might not be believed; that's why they had hid, allowing the Russians to scout things out.

Once again, opinions diverged about what attitude to adopt. Some, who backed Armand, wanted to set up the execution stake immediately; others thought they were sincere and would make trustworthy allies. Between the two were those who hesitated: it was best to wait a little, spy on them, interrogate them, find out what they really wanted. A voice rose above that confused discussion.

"Let's begin by searching the damned Germans!"

"Good idea," answered Addi Bâ, a bit ashamed at not having thought of that earlier.

That is when the insignificant incident occurred that was to be the end of Camp Deliverance and determine your uncle's fate.

There were neither arms nor spy devices, but in amidst the lighters, the military papers, the broken cigarettes, and biscuit crumbs, Bertrand found a shiny object.

"Gosh, a watch, a gold watch! I can keep it, can't I, Sergeant? I can keep it?"

"Of course, Bertrand, it'll be your war booty."

"I'm the one who arrested them, Sir. I deserve to keep the watch," said Armand.

"I gave it to Bertrand. I'm not going to take it away from him, Armand!"

"It isn't fair, Sir, it isn't fair!"

Then he muttered something and disappeared into the barracks.

"What did he say, Bertrand?"

"I couldn't hear him, Sir."

"He said, 'This won't be the end of it,'" answered another boy.

"Stop acting like a child, Armand! Soon, all of Germany will be your war booty! All right; off to bed, boys! Bertrand, you're in charge of the camp, and Armand, you watch over the prisoners!"

When he left, he was planning on going to talk to Simon or to his "mama." He was faced with a difficult dilemma, and he needed someone to help him assess and resolve it. He met up with Simon and Yolande in one of their usual hiding places, after using the agreed-upon signals and passwords. They discussed what should be done at Camp Deliverance for hours. At the crack of dawn, Simon, not feeling comfortable making military decisions, suggested asking Gauthier's opinion, whereas Yolande, following her feminine instinct, wished to spare the lives of those poor men.

The mother and son rode their bicycles side by side till they reached Petit-Bourg, where Addi Bâ stopped.

"You know very well I can't go any farther," he said.

"Fine, see you tomorrow!"

"You're not going to give me a hug?"

"Yes, of course, little fellow! And do your best to watch out for those poor Germans, so that nothing happens to them until their fate can be decided upon."

"I'm Commander of the Resistance fighters, Mama. I alone can decide."

"And what will you decide?"

"Top secret, Mama. All right, good night!"

The next night, he reached the camp and, even before getting off his bike, screamed, "Bring out the prisoners, and put up the stake!"

Bertrand walked toward him trembling and handed him a small bit of paper. He read it and in a hushed, panic-stricken voice ordered, "Shit, hide the firearms, burn the camp down, then scatter!"

This is what the paper said: *Sir, you know perfectly well that the watch was my due!*

The prisoners had escaped.

"Bertrand, get Armand out here!"

"Armand, isn't here anymore. He's disappeared too, Sir."

He got back on his bicycle and hurried toward Petit-Bourg and Lamarche, in order to put up the distress signals for Yolande and Simon. Then he went and locked himself in his house.

He wasn't aware that in Vittel and Epinal, the Jerries were rushing out of their barracks and fanning out all over the region.

They surrounded the Boène farm around four o'clock in the morning and ordered Gaston Houillon, the owner, to take them to Camp Deliverance. The good Vosgian farmer made as if to obey, but took them in the opposite direction, toward the road to La Vacheresse. That gave his daughters time to warn Bertrand and the two other boys that were still up there not to hang around the Partisans' Oak. Paulette and Jeannine, who were only fourteen and sixteen years old, picked up their staffs, pretending to go out to bring in the cows.

They went up and told the boys, "Run for it—the Germans are at our place!"

"You're lying!"

The poor kids didn't believe the girls. The Jerries captured all three of them and dragged them in front of Mrs. Houillon (who'd had the presence of mind to throw the roneo into the manure pit).

"Is this your son, Madame?" they asked, pointing to Bertrand.

"Of course not," she answered, trying to hide the fear that was making her voice quaver.

The poor woman knew that her son Albert was behind the house hiding under a large elder bush. From there, believing his last hour had come, he observed the Germans' incursion, watched as they searched the attic and the garden, swarmed along the road to La Vacheresse, and hid out in all the woods from the Mouzon plain to Camp Deliverance.

He thought they'd burned down the village and slit his parents' throats. It was hell, Mister, sheer hell! And then, in the blinding hot sun, a six-foot-five giant appeared, proud of his stature, his handsome uniform, and his machine gun. He walked over toward the rabbit hutch a few meters away, knelt down, his finger on the trigger. That lasted for an hour, maybe two. If Albert had coughed or sneezed during that time, he would have ended up like Bertrand and his two companions, who died of exhaustion in a concentration camp somewhere in Bavaria or Moldavia.

The sisters finally brought in the cows, but the Germans continued to flood in. After the milking, everyone had to be served: one hundred liters of milk gulped down in a few seconds, and they would have asked for more if the Houillons had had more cows.

Then the soldiers came back down from Camp Deliverance with the firearms they'd seized. Amongst them were the two Germans and the Russians who'd said they were deserters along with that infamous Alfred fellow, the dubious proprietor of Le Café de l'Univers. They requisitioned Gaston and his horse and wagon to take everything to the town hall in La Villotte. After their departure, Albert coughed, and his mother understood immediately: she brought him out some food and a pair of pincers. He cut open the fence and slithered on his belly like a snake to make his way into the woods, where he hid for a few days. When the pack of Gestapo officers thinned out, he followed the hunting paths and the forest galleries and reached Switzerland, where he hired himself out as a farmhand until the Liberation of Paris.

At the same time the group of *essesses* was investing the Boène farm, the heart of the tragedy was unfolding right here in Romaincourt, over there in the old house standing before you, which has remained uninhabited since that dark day.

It was July and I'd just come back from Paris for summer vacation.

I was awakened by the sounds of motors and barking dogs. It all happened in just a few seconds, a few seconds that are still not over, a few seconds that represent a century for me, a few seconds that have brought you all the way here from across the seas.

They surrounded the house, busted down the door, and rushed up to his room, filling the air with the clattering of their boots. Addi Bâ jumped out the window and tried to flee through the orchard.

A shot rang out, he fell to the ground—the bullet had hit his tibia.

Who betrayed Addi Bâ? Asmodée? Cyprien Rapenne? That hothead Armand Demange? Or was it one of his many lovers?

His life as a Don Juan remains as enigmatic as his life as a Resistance fighter, and he led both of them down to their most minute details, as if they were secret missions. You'll hear about the farmer woman from Roncourt, the nurse from Martigny-les-Bains, the widow from Fouchécourt, and that's about it. From time to time, someone will bring up the infamous Zenette without daring to stick his neck out too far. We saw her for the first time after the Liberation of Paris when, head shaven and covered with spittle, she was paraded around half-naked along with other traitors, like that Alfred fellow from Le Café de l'Univers, where Simon had first encountered Gauthier.

You could see she'd been beautiful and rich in another life, but few people know why she began to neglect herself.

She popped up at the beginning of the war, rented that sumptuous house over by Robécourt from which, by night, the sound of music and ringing laughter would often escape.

Addi Bâ started going there in the very first days of Camp Deliverance, around March of 1943. He went there because the food was excellent (dishes served nowhere else save to the Germans, and sometimes the Colonel). He went because, in addition to Robert Marino, there was also modern music that had recently come flooding into Europe from Argentina, Martinique, or Trinidad and Tobago. But above all, he went there for her, for her snake-like eyes, for her tight perfumed dresses.

He only went on Thursdays and not until around midnight. She would grab him as soon as he came in the door and wrap her tentacles around him. They would fall on to the sofa, roll around on the carpet, catch their breaths, have a bite to eat, dance a tango, and begin all over again.

After that, they'd listen to "Tango de Marilou" over and over again. He'd sip on his tea; she'd pour herself a glass of vermouth with such grace as had never been seen in this part of France. They spoke of Paris, mentioned the Folies Bergères and the Bal Nègre. She was eloquent on the subject. Whereas with that Asmodée bitch, everything was forced: her clothing and her mannerisms were never able to cover up her commonplace character and provincial origins.

Zenette spent her weekends at the sanatorium in Bourbonne-les-Bains, which the Germans had requisitioned for their field officers shortly after they arrived here.

Once a month, a man came from Paris in his Citroën, sporting magnificent gabardine suits, bringing pictures of Pétain. After the Liberation, his photo would make headlines on the darkest pages of France's history.

I know all of this thanks to Antoine Palet, who worked as a waiter in the bar at the sanatorium back then and whose services Zenette would sometimes call upon to liven up her private parties. The officer she went to see there was called Häffpen, the Baron Tobiass von Häffpen. A young, courteous, and refined general who had a passion for French culture and was a great admirer of Napoleon. He owned a miniature of the emperor, a piece confiscated from a rich collector in Vittel that he'd acquired in an auction organized by the Feldkommandantur for the profit of German war widows.

He would have his suite cleaned, the carpets and the flowers changed to prepare for Zenette's visit. He was so gallant that upon her arrival he would take down the portrait of the Führer and put the representation of Bonaparte in its place. That was what betrayed poor Zenette, because the precious piece was found at her place after the German army fled.

That doesn't mean she alone was the cause of your uncle's demise. Oh, no! The collaborators were far more numerous, more widespread, far more underhanded, and better organized than the Resistance. Neighbors were spied upon, cousins or uncles were denounced, friends were hunted down for a measly package of cigarettes. Those days were a dream come true for that spiteful clan of Rapenne trash.

Cyprien Rapenne had written anonymous letters informing on Nonon Totor, you know that already. On the other hand, you don't know that after his chicken coop burned down, he'd gone on a bender and later went and talked with those *cheûlard*-boozers at Chez Marie.

"It's a dirty Tergoresse trick. The bastards! I'm going to get that nigger of theirs burned!"

A Tergoresse trick, when in summer sparks float about of their own accord in Romaincourt, what with the charcoal everyone makes in their backyards and the ovens on every street corner for heating up irons.

As for Armand Demange, no one ever heard tell of him again. People still wonder what really happened on that cursed day the devil decided to strike down Camp Deliverance. Did the prisoners escape? Had Armand—being the terribly proud person we knew him to be—vanished into thin air to hide his shame at having neglected his duty? If he'd purposefully let them go, does that mean he was in cahoots with them?

No one has yet succeeded in answering those questions. One thing remains certain: not one compromising piece of evidence concerning him was found either in the closets of the Feldkommandantur or the basements of the Gestapo. Many people think it can all be chalked up to the mistakes of a young kid who misunderstood his time, a kid who'd come straight out from under his mama's skirts and didn't know that childish impulsiveness could cause tragedies.

When the Americans landed and tricolor flags began waving over French soil, all that remained for us to do was empty out the closets and lick our wounds. What we saw was not a pretty sight, Mister. The archives found in the rubble of the Feldkommandantur stunk to high heaven! It stunk of people like Asmodée, like Cyprien Rapenne and so many other dirty rats who'd left their tracks there.

Except no men were lapidated, no women's heads were shaved in Romaincourt. In Romaincourt we don't punish people, Mister. We shut things up in a wall of silence and resentment, we trust in the Lord Jesus and in time to allow the curse to finish its work.

Five years after the Liberation, Asmodée dragged herself limping to see the priest, wearing a black veil.

"I've come to clean up."

"Clean up what, the dust or your sins?"

"Both, Father."

That answer still rings in the ears of the people of Romaincourt as an admission that her life had been consumed by lust, lies, and criminal acts. From that day until her death, she seconded me at the church, not lackadaisically, not reluctantly, never bringing up the past. She would leave Pinéguette at the school or in the back courtyard of the church with her toys. Under my direction, she would wash the front steps, dust off the altar and the confessional booth, put away the candleholders and the prayer stools.

That lasted for a year, then one evening as she was walking home, she discovered her daughter collapsed in the washhouse, her toys scattered along the main street, her underpants torn to shreds, and her thighs streaming with blood while the gendarmes went rushing into the woods hot on the trail of Cyprien Rapenne.

So I slipped into his room to save his documents while the Jerries were working him over, shoving him this way and that until they dragged him from the orchard to the front steps of the church. It reminded us of the time he'd fallen off his bicycle, Mister, because he was near death and everyone in Romaincourt was watching the scene, despite the dogs, despite the hostility of the Germans soldiers who were meting out blows with their rifle butts and *hachepaillant*, as we say, barking out guttural orders. We'd never seen them so worked up before.

"Der schwarze Terrorist! Der schwarze Terrorist! The black terrorist! The black terrorist!"

They were running around in all directions. They searched his room and the mayor's offices, deployed their soldiers in ominous military marches while he lay in his own blood with his eyes closed and beads of sweat on his forehead. Nonon Totor walked over to him with a pitcher of fresh water. One of the *essesses* aimed his revolver and shattered it.

"No water for *terrorischtes*! Is that clear?" he belched out at the top of his lungs.

"Clear as..."

My Nonon Totor didn't finish his sentence, and no one will ever know whether he meant to say "crystal" or "the nose on a Jerry's face." Tears as large as trickles of faucet water were running down his unrecognizable cheeks. That was the day he met with sorrow, that nasty creature which never lets go, once it's got hold. From that day on, I never saw him smile or heard him joke around again, right up to that blasted afternoon in 1950 when he was found on the banks of the Mouzon, having succumbed to a peaceful heart attack while practicing the favorite pastime he'd tried in vain to instill in your uncle: line fishing.

It lasted into the middle of the morning, they hastily bandaged his wounds and threw him into a patrol wagon. Romaincourt watched him go, and everyone—Papa, Mama, Nonon Totor, the mayor, Mâmiche Léontine, the Colonel—all of us knew we'd never see him again. When the cruel convoy disappeared around the bend of the main street, we each walked mournfully back to our respective homes in silence.

We didn't yet know that they'd just arrested Yolande Valdenaire in Petit-Bourg and thrown her into a train bound for Germany.

Young Etienne retained his innocent gaze and his generous smile even after he learned his mother would never return—lost forever to that camp in Saxony known as Bautzen, where she'd been sent to die a slow death. Neither did he take it poorly when an ambulance came to cart his father away to the asylum. Awakening one morning to the crack of rifle shots, Petit-Bourg was astonished to find Hubert Valdenaire perched high in a tree, shooting at hay carts and anything else that moved on the road that ran past his house.

A few months later, Etienne decided to settle in Paris, where he'd just been offered a job as a printer and where I was to join him after his first year of salary. He gave me a long kiss and said good-bye to everyone without showing the slightest twinge of regret or resentment.

He's the type of man who goes through life without a bruise, without a scratch. He must have a second appendix inside to trap the bad parts of life and protect him from their harmful effects. Not everyone is able to live eighty years in the Vosges and not bear a grudge against God or the human race. Oh, he has his little weaknesses, just as everyone does: from time to time, he'll sulk or get angry; from time to time, you'll catch a glint of sadness or melancholy deep in his eye. And then there are those scatterbrained incidents that drive him to do something altogether different from what he set out to do. But no one would hold that against him. On the contrary, you feel sorry for him when the time comes for him to pay the price of his mistake.

You won't believe me, Mister, but when he announced he'd fallen madly in love and it was all over between us, most of the pain I felt was for him. Of course I was hurt; of course I would've liked to keep him for myself. But I thought of him during the two weeks I spent closed up in my room crying. Did he really love her? Did she love him too? Would she make him happy? Would she prove to be worthy of him? Could she live up to his intelligence, his sensitivity, and his generosity?

You probably think I rejoiced when I learned of his divorce. Well no, Mister, I didn't, no, I didn't! I'd rather see him happy, even if it has to be without me.

Over there in Australia, he must feel very remote from all of this, and my only wish is that the good Lord Jesus will finally open the doors to happiness for him. He'll live a long time, that Etienne—he's made for living, he's made to be happy. Etienne knows a good deal about happiness, despite the bitter fruit, despite the thorns.

You can't say as much for that Pinéguette. She came into the world through the wrong door, Mister. With the mother she had, the good Lord Jesus couldn't do much of anything for her. She was bound to suffer and grow up far from his blessed hand, far from his salutary light. From the moment of her birth, she had to make her way through foul, joyless, and loveless seas, never having even an inkling of inner peace. She was born for that alone, suffering, suffering, wriggling about night and day in shadows and in sin. Receiving and doling out blows, that's all she knew how to do. And it wasn't her fault, Mister, no—she would have been a good soul if it hadn't been for Asmodée's cursed belly. Deep down, that Pinéguette wasn't all that bad. She sent me a nice little card from Holland just before she was smashed up in that international motorcycle rally where she thought she'd win her fourth cup for speed racing.

If she'd been here, oh yes, if she'd been here, she would have seen that magnificent plaque and been happy for the first time in her life.

I waited for two weeks, just time enough to pull myself back together. Then I prepared a lunch pail and stood in front of La Prison de la Vierge in Epinal. I followed the long red-brick walls bristling with barbed wire and watchtowers, but I wasn't brave enough to go up to the entrance gate, feeling intimidated by the uniforms of the sentinels, the constant comings and goings of platoons, of motor tricycles and tanks. I stood hiding behind a post three yards away, determined to have my little pot of food admitted, or lose my life trying.

I closed my eyes, clenched my fists, breathed in as much air as my lungs could hold to bolster my courage. I began counting: one, two, three... Just then I felt a breath on my neck.

"What are you doing here, Miss?"

It was a young man of my age. He took off his beret when I turned to face him and tapped me on the shoulder to help me catch my breath.

"I quite scared you there, now didn't I? So what are you doing here? I assure you this is no place to be hanging around."

"I... I've brought him some food."

"Who?"

"Addi Bâ!"

"The black man? They'll never let it through, Miss. He's the most heavily guarded of all. They call him the 'black terrorist.' *Der schwarze Terrorist!*"

"Do you know him?"

"Of course not, but I see him from time to time. I'm the prison barber. I see them all, sometimes several times a week."

His name was Henri, Henri Maubert. He took me by the hand and led me away from there, to a spot under the Sadi-Cornot Bridge, where no one could hear us.

"It's not a pretty sight up there, I can guarantee you that, Miss."

"At least they're lucky enough to have a barber."

"But Miss, the hair is for making blankets and lining for their boots—did you think it was to pretty them up?"

"What are they accusing him of?"

"Of having created a Resistance group, a terrorist camp, if you prefer. And do you know what? He's not alone: there are at least three others accused of the same crime."

"Who else?"

"Gaston Houillon from the Boène farm and Marcel Arbuger, the one they used to call Simon. Old Gaston has already been sentenced: six months for aiding and abetting. There's a good chance the other two will receive a more severe sentence."

"I thought he'd gotten away."

"Marcel Arbuger? They caught him in Dijon—someone informed on him. And the other man, the one called Froitier, is thought to have escaped into the Hautes-Vosges. They've got men on his trail."

"Did they confess?"

"No, and that's precisely what makes it so tragic. They're pretending not to know one another, for how long? You know, a few hours in there and all traces of humanity disappear.

"They're not torturing them, are they?"

"Torturing isn't done here but at Gestapo headquarters. They leave in the morning. They put them on a billiard table and use instruments of all sorts and shapes, one for each part of the body."

Mama went to try her luck too, taking radishes, cheese, a delicious *frichti* of chicken thighs and apples from the orchard that he used to enjoy picking so much, whistling our traditional tunes. Then it was Mâmiche Léontine's turn, then Papa, then the mayor, and then Nonon Totor and the Colonel... no one being any more successful than I was.

We hadn't even realized that summer was already over.

" *Môn*, my God," exclaimed Nonon Totor, "it's been three months now! They must be a sorry sight, after eating garbage and conversing with the rats. I'll never speak German as long as I live, you hear?"

We soon realized how useless it was for us to become indignant. Drowned in the dreary gray of fall, drowned in Romaincourt's day-to-day monotony, we imagined in silence what they must have been going through over there.

I watched, as if in a film, the van come back from the Gestapo, the grill open and then close again, the crowd of men in tatters climb out under a rain of insults and rifle blows—of course he was the very last one to drag himself out. It wasn't because he was black that we recognized him—they'd all turned black from having rolled around in excrement, from never washing—but because of his limp and the traces of puss and blood he left behind. Henri had told me they weren't treating him, or at least so summarily that his wound had gangrened and he had to use both hands to lift his foot.

I can picture him tearing off pieces of his prison garment to improvise bandages. Someone moaning in the neighboring cell, his trying in vain to comfort him. I imagine him receiving a message slipped under his door by a fellow prisoner, by the barber, perhaps by a German soldier, but he can't understand a word, he's unable to read it, his eyes can no longer focus, his mind refuses to think.

What had become of Yolande? We didn't know, and he even less so.

And Gaston Houillon? And Marcel Arbuger? Right across the hall, or to the left just a few steps away... Perhaps sunk in a coma, perhaps dead... Impossible to smile at one another, impossible to give a wink or a slap on the shoulder when they passed each other in the mess or in the torture chamber. Most painful of all was acting as if they didn't know each other, had never seen each other. Showing the slightest sign of recognition would have meant that somewhere else, people would have struggled for nothing...

I dreamed that something would happen before the summer holidays were over: something marvelous, something reassuring, something luminous and new, something that would arrive like a sign from the heavens to tell me it was time to go back to Paris: a miraculous amnesty, a small opportunity for evasion...

No, not on your life, nothing but darkness and hard luck! Dear God up in heaven surely must have switched off the lights and the sound as well...

On December 3, 1943, Addi Bâ and Marcel Arbuger were condemned to death. They were executed on the morning of December 18, such a foggy morning that—according to Henri Maubert—you could see the wings of angels fluttering against the church steeples of Epinal.

Lightning Source UK Ltd.
Milton Keynes UK
UKOW01f1402081116
287063UK00012B/19/P